Rudolf von Gott

Withered Leaves
Volume 1

Rudolf von Gottschall

Withered Leaves
Volume 1

1st Edition | ISBN: 978-3-75232-710-6

Place of Publication: Frankfurt am Main, Germany

Year of Publication: 2020

Outlook Verlag GmbH, Germany.

WITHERED LEAVES.

BY

Rudolf von Gottschall.

VOL. I.

CHAPTER I.

ON THE FUCHS-SPITZE.

Large and full stood the moon in the eastern sky, and reflected its broken light in the troubled waves which the Baltic Sea cast upon the coast of Samland; it silvered the tangled thicket of the ravine through which here and there quivered a ray of the woodland stream, with its scanty supply of water, as with difficulty it forced its way amongst the stones onward to the ocean. The primordiate blocks of granite, which kept watch at the estuary of the streamlet, gained a venerable appearance in the light of the planets; but more venerable still appeared the primeval oaks of Perkunos, with their silvery tips, as they rose upon the rocky projection, and down whose lightning-struck stems the moonlight glided softly.

Was it a priestess of the old heathen deities who stood there, in her light robe, leaning against the trunk of the mightiest oak, her gaze turned outwards upon the wide sea, whose opposite breakers washed the land of the ancient Vikings? But no! The heathen priestesses, who sacrificed at the oaks of their gods, were venerable women, while that slender figure bore all the witchery of youth, and looked much too gentle for such a horrible craft! So much spiritual tenderness lay in her large, widely-opened gazelle-like eyes, and besides—many, many centuries ago the days of Paganism had passed away, even although then, as now, the waves beat upon the strand, and the tops of the oaks rustled, for we live in the nineteenth century; old Herkus Monte and the other Nathang and Samland leaders of armies have long since been replaced by the commanders of the King of Prussia's regiments and battalions, and for two years this coast, like the whole land of Prussia, has been ruled over by that spirited Hohenzollern Prince, Friedrich Wilhelm IV.

"How it blows," said the Regierungsrath, as he buttoned his overcoat more closely, "I do not love these evening amusements; I find that the sea makes a much deeper impression by day, and then, one does not expose oneself to the danger of paying for these so-called enjoyments of nature with rheumatic pains."

"But, my husband," replied the Regierungsräthin, a fine woman, a thorough Lithuanian, whose cradle stood on the shores of Memel, "you are indeed too prosaic! One must just for once see the ocean by moonlight; besides Evchen has cherished this wish for long. Two weeks already have we been in Warnicken, and always have gone to bed as the moon rose."

"We do not go in for marine painting," replied the Regierungsrath drily, as his chin disappeared farther and farther into his enormous white cravat, "and Eva, too, will take cold. The girl has a delicate constitution; you, dear wife, judge all the world by yourself; but we are not all so fortunate as to possess weather-proof giant natures. How the girl stands there in her light summer dress! Eva, wrap your shawl round you, a cold breeze from the north is blowing."

The girl awoke as if from a dream, she wrapped herself obediently in the shawl that she carried upon her arm, and hastened towards her father and mother, who were standing against the foremost railing of the projection.

"Oh, how beautiful, how enchantingly beautiful it is here," cried Eva, with her heart full, and tears standing in her eyes, tears such as only youth can shed in overflowing moods, when the charm of nature presciently awakes gloomy feelings in the heart.

The Regierungsrath could not explain these tears to himself, because every rational cause for them was wanting, and indeed every irrational one; any kind of wish denied would speedily have solved the mystery for him. Therefore he made the cold wind responsible, and folded his daughter still more closely in her shawl. Her mother, on the contrary, who had equally little sympathy with such-like emotional outbreaks, but knew better how to divine their cause, cried, reprovingly—

"Learn to wean yourself from over-sensitiveness, dear child! How often already have I been obliged to tell you so! You must learn gradually to control your feelings. All this is very beautiful: moonshine and ocean's tide, groups of trees and wooded vallies, and the steep precipitous rocks; yet one must not admire it too much; it is after all an old tale, and one must not appear too new to the world. What would people say to it? At some period one must leave school behind, and enter into life."

Eva pressed herself deprecatingly against her mother, whose gigantic form towered above the slender girl; but her father, after having taken a pinch of snuff, assumed a complacent tone of voice, and began to expound his views as to the capabilities of profit possessed by the Samland sea-bathing places. Eva had ample leisure to survey the beautiful picture of the moonlight evening, to follow the lines of the surf-surrounded coasts to the uttermost foreland, and ever again to lower her gaze into the mystery of the Wolf's schlucht, above which the most luxuriant vegetation rose and fell like green breakers in the sough of the night wind.

Then voices suddenly arose from the paths which led upward through the wood to the Fuchs-spitze; they were not the melodies of strolling singers, but the music of artists. One female voice, by its beautiful full tone, made itself conspicuous amongst all the others, and that singer's execution appeared to be by no means inconsiderable. The Regierungsrath found this interruption to his discourse the more disagreeable, because he was about to make a few propositions by which sea-bathing places, such as this romantic Warnicken, could be raised out of their rude primitive condition into fashionable watering places.

In the meanwhile the party of male and female singers had reached the summit, their hats and coats garlanded with wreaths of leaves. They appeared to be in a most lively mood, and broke out into loud rejoicings when they had gained the point whence a view could be obtained; some clapped their hands, and at a signal, which an elderly gentleman gave with a walking-stick used as a conductor's *bâton*, all began to sing a most artistically correct *Jodler*. In the faces and in the whole demeanour of the party there lay that peculiarity by which actors and actresses are unmistakable even in their exterior; an air of mental freedom, the assurance and self-sufficiency of manner, and at the same time the appearance of struggling after an ideal, which even those know how to maintain who follow their art as a rather rude handicraft. In fact, they were singers from the provincial capital, who were wandering along the shore for a holiday excursion, but had set up their head-quarters in the favourite seaside watering place Cranz, which by its sociable doings atoned for what its desolate strand lacked in natural beauty.

It soon became apparent that the most prominent female person in the group, a tall figure with southern glowing eyes, with noble aristocratic features, and dark hair that shone amongst the green oak branches with the polish of ebony, was that accomplished singer, who, during the party's ascent, had borne away the prize of song. Leaning over the balustrade, she warbled a melody into the night air, with trills and cadences irreproachably executed, while the fuller notes were uttered with most soul-felt intensity of expression.

"Bravo, Signora Bollini!" cried the elderly gentleman, who had previously waved the *bâton*, "even the most unfavourable critic, the most venomous monster that lurks in any newspaper's crevice, would be obliged to write a laudatory criticism upon this performance. Besides you are in wonderfully good voice."

"You know, dear Conductor," replied the Signora, "that I possess an impressionable soul; here in free beautiful nature I regulate my powers quite differently from what I do when I stand behind you at the piano, looking down upon its venerable smooth surface, and the pages of music upon the lifeless paper, that I am to transpose into ringing coin. One must have

4

illusions, best of conductors; but to sing to order, at the appointed time, as announced on the black board, for wages which themselves sometimes belong to illusions, takes away all inclination, and acts most depressingly upon one's mind. Art can only thrive in freedom!"

"It is well known to us all," said the Conductor, "that our beautiful *prima donna* belongs to those natures, which, in the language of art, may be designated as *cappricciose*, and which only with difficulty can accustom themselves to any regular walk in life, or indeed to any rules of business."

"Now you are talking of business again," said the Signora, "naming art and business in one breath, it is enough to make all the muses take to flight!"

"Well, well," replied the Director, "everything in the world will have its season, and as regards business, *prime donne* do not understand that so badly when honorariums for their performances, or profitable paragraphs, are concerned."

"Not seldom, dear Master," said the singer, with a winning expression of countenance, which suddenly became somewhat gentler, and more amiable. That which she had said about her impressionability, had been confirmed by the rapid change of her face's expression; yes, it betokened cordial acquiescence, most unhesitating reciprocation of everything that was friendly; the greatest readiness to follow the other's moods, the trains of thought, certainly as it seemed, without that reserve which stricter womanliness required, as the flattering speeches by which she now sought to assuage the Conductor, contained something syren-like; every word was a caress, and only slight mockery, which sometimes echoed from them, showed that no real affection prompted their utterance.

This party was very disagreeable to the Regierungsrath; he did not love art, he liked to avoid all artists; in his eyes closer intercourse with them did not appear suitable to his position and he was glad to withdraw himself from the brotherly manner in which the disciples of art seek to place themselves on a footing of equality with all other mortals. He was on the point of taking flight from the Fuchs-spitze, which had suddenly become a Parnassus to him, when he was prevented doing so by the greeting of a young man, who released himself from the oak-leaf-wreathed group and stepped towards him.

"Good evening, Herr Regierungsrath Kalzow," rang the cordial greeting accompanied by a hearty shake of the hand, with which the female members of the Kalzow family were also favoured.

"Ah, Herr Doctor Schöner," replied the Rath, "what brings you here, then, in such jovial company?"

"You know," replied the young Doctor of Law, "that the ministry puts a stop to my political career, will not grant me the *venia legendi* at the University. Thus I have been obliged to exchange the useful for the agreeable; I have dedicated myself as dramatic scenery assistant to the theatre, and belong to a certain extent to the strolling troupe. We have just come from Memel, where we stirred up the Jack tars to enthusiasm with our melodies; then we waded through the sand of the Kurische Nehrung; sailed across the waters of the Kurische Haff in a smoking steamboat and settled down domestically in Cranz. The opera namely, and I, who although I really live on very bad terms with the trebles and general bass, yet am more enthusiastic about the operatic than the dramatic company, and at least enjoy my holidays with the former; the ballet, too, is represented here! Look, that languishing lady there is our *première danseuse*, does she not look something like one of the moon's rays that had been left behind? Each of her *pas* is a danced sigh. None of these ladies will receive a part through me; therefore I believe in the disinterestedness of their love glances."

The Doctor had only made these confessions to the Rath. Eva, with her mother, had retreated farther into the shadowy net of a Perkunos oak; but suddenly a peculiar pallor lay upon her features.

Young Schöner was well known to her; she had often seen and spoken to him in a friend's house, and as he strove very eagerly to gain her good-will, she had not remained perfectly indifferent to him.

Indeed, he might well win a girlish heart by his uncommon character. He behaved much more romantically than all adherents of art; his velvet coat, certainly, had been neat and glossy when it came from the tailor; yet it was terribly receptive of everything that flies about in the air, and soon lost all its charms of freshness.

A wide, turned-down shirt collar, without any intervening neckerchief, lay extended over his shoulders, like linen upon a bleaching-ground; a student's velvet cap sat defiantly upon his brow, even although it had now forfeited the silver Albertus, the proud badge of the academical citizens of Albertina, and the thorn stick in his hand quite answered to that one which the "wild man" carries in popular pictures.

His long black hair, however, which fell down upon his shoulders, enframed an interesting face, which was sharply, but not badly cut, and was surmounted by a pair of fiery and remarkable eyes.

The young Doctor, indeed, was an aspiring young fellow, and had allowed several poetical larks to rise, whose warbling notes had been heard afar through Germany.

At two-and-twenty years of age he was a species of celebrity, and celebrity is often the easily-obtained fruit of fashion. At that time everything was the fashion that came from the Baltic shore, where the beacons of political freedom blazed.

Thus young Doctor Schöner was deemed a genius—that is a strong letter of recommendation to a young girl, who has just left school—and, therefore, even the keen female eye does not perceive those tiny specks upon the velvet coat and that unfashionable hair, which detests the scissors.

The young poet now went towards Eva, and commenced a conversation with her about the beauty of the evening, and the beauties in the party of actresses, extolling Signora Bollini with glowing eulogy.

Eva, who leaned against the trunk of the giant oak, would have liked best to hide herself in it like a dryad, so as not to be obliged to listen to this praise, not to look at this goddess of art.

"Doctorchen, whither have you vanished?" suddenly rang the Signora's mellifluous voice, audible far around, and stepping nearer, she said, with a graceful inclination towards mother and daughter: "Ah, with the blue-bell, in the shadow of the sacred oak! You must spare my amanuensis tome to-day, ladies. He knows the road, the path, the names of all the hills on the coast, and the little bays—he is my map."

At the Signora's first words, Schöner had retreated from Eva, as though he had been caught upon forbidden paths. He introduced the ladies to one another, and immediately disappeared amongst the group of actors.

After a few polite words, which she had exchanged with the Regierungsrath's family, the Signora was back again in the midst of her own people.

Again a bright song resounded, accompanied by the waves breaking still louder on the shore.

Annoyed at the long stay, the Regierungsrath gave the signal to return home, and as they departed Eva could still hear the singer's merry words.

"Now ladies, away into the surging tide! Who would not wish to be a moonlight-water-fairy for once? I feel like a spirit of the elements, and my adorers have long since declared me to be an Undine, because in their opinion I have no soul. All the same—souls are the cheapest things in the world, and the smallest State has many hundreds of thousands of them! Besides, one must be able to exist without a soul, if one can only offer some substitute for it."

"Bravo!" cried Schöner; "long live our Undine!"

"Therefore, gentlemen, *abonnement suspendu* for the Baltic Sea? To-night it belongs to the ladies, and you return quietly to the hotel. You need have no fear that I shall transform myself down below in the breaking surf into a Melusina, and perhaps, coquette with a fish's tail. I am no silvery-scaled monster, but both on land and in water a woman *comme il faut. En avant,* ladies! Here are no hearses as in Cranz; here one springs from the shore into the waves, and the only Actæon who plays the spy upon us is the moon! It shall have its horns; it will soon enter upon its last quarter!"

Ladies and gentlemen descended the Fuchs-spitze on separate paths.

Eva had not lost a word of the singer's speech; it caused her to shiver uncomfortably, and she wrapped herself more closely in her shawl.

"An intolerable party," said the Regierungsrath to his wife; "so bold, so impudent."

"I do not understand," replied she, "how young Doctor Schöner can find pleasure in it."

"I understand it quite well! It is just the society for such ill-regulated minds! He would never have been fitted for a political career; it is not that he has no head, but everything ferments and surges in him in wild confusion."

"Perhaps he would settle down in time."

"Never! A thorn bends itself early to the form which it is to assume, and an official must bend himself betimes; I mean by this, control and govern himself, as we have only one gospel, that of duty!"

"He is thoughtless with girls, too; without exception, he pays attention to all, if they only belong in any degree to the fair sex. Evchen, you have met him at Justizrath Spillner's; he is said to have distinguished you, too."

Eva bent down and gathered a large-belled campanula, which grew by the roadside.

"It is fortunate," said the Regierungsrath, "that he has not yet dared to enter our house; in his poetry he has uttered such thoughts for the world's reform, that I should fall into bad odour with the whole of my colleagues, if he forced himself into my society."

"Perhaps he fears the same with his good friends," replied the Regierungsräthin, shrugging her shoulders; "as these so-called Liberals make their comments also, and we are certainly in their bad books."

"It is incredible, but you may be right. What have we not had to experience since our King's accession to the throne! Parties are formed, there is an Opposition, and we, who until now only had to command in order to meet with obedience, are confronted by resistance! Any young Doctor of Law thinks he can dictate to a President of Council what he is to do or leave undone."

"Calm yourself, my dear husband! In return he is in this *prima donna's* fetters, and he must obey her signs, as you have seen, and be a slave to her. A beautiful woman, certainly!"

"I did not look so closely at her."

"I know better, old man! I believe you could write her passport, mentioning all her peculiar marks of distinction. It does not matter! There is no danger in it, as she only seeks young admirers; I wager that Doctor Schöner's baptismal certificate is dated a few years after hers."

"I do not comprehend," said Kalzow, "how any man can place himself under the command of a feminine being! What becomes of manly dignity in such a case?"

At these words the Regierungsrath brought out a cigar-case so as to light himself a Havannah cigar.

"What are you doing, old man? How often have I already told you that you shall not smoke a cigar in the evening just before going to bed! It does not agree with you, the Doctor advised you not to do it; I forbid it positively in his name."

While speaking these words the Frau Regierungsräthin drew herself up to her full height.

"Then, at least, I will have another glass of beer over there."

"Nothing! That too is injurious for you! In other matters you are quite right! It is a disgrace to bow to the orders of such a theatrical princess; but to obey a sensible woman has never brought evil or dishonour."

Amid such conversations the family had reached the small fisherman's cottage in which they lived; Eva soon went to her attic-chamber, locked the door, opened the window and looked out into the moonlight night. Silently she had listened to her parents' discussion; only a few days ago she had taken young Doctor Schöner under her protection against all accusations, to-day she could do so no longer! She had been credulous enough to believe the Doctor's words of flattery; had he not distinguished her amongst her girl friends! As yet no word of love had been spoken, but a liking for the gifted young man had found utterance in her heart.

People talk so much of first and only love—and yet, if one looks closer into it, all kinds of budding affections, which never attain their full development, precede this first love; near the first rose there are plenty of buds which hang broken and faded on the stalk; many side-chapels where love erects itself modest altars, are forsaken before it strides to the high one in the great nave of the church. And no girl leaves sixteen or seventeen years behind her, without having obtained in a brother's friend, in a neighbour, in a *vis-à-vis*, a small ideal for the preliminary studies of love. There is a heart's idolatry even in earliest youth; yet the roots of such affections only rest loosely in the lightest soil.

Eva's first attempt at love was devoted to the young Doctor; she had erected a little temple for him in her heart, and adorned his picture with many floral wreaths of tender feelings. It is true her friends had often cautioned her in joke against the homage of the fickle poet; she ascribed it to envy, which even amongst young female friends is not a rarity. But now she had seen, with her own eyes, how he had bestowed his admiration upon another proud beauty, yes wandered with her through the country; she had heard how confidently that other had asserted her rights over him; it had dealt a stab to her heart, and it was a consolation for her, when her father and mother expressed themselves so hostilely towards him: a defiant feeling became powerful within her, she would hear nothing more from him, release herself entirely from him, drive away his picture as one wipes a dream out of one's eyes.

Yet slightly below the surface as the roots of a love, in this case not at all serious, had struck, it was a mixture of bitter and painful emotions which besieged the girl's heart, as it dug up its first shy affection.

Was that not the roar of the sea that sounded from afar? Was it not the proud Melusina who sang as she bathed her beautiful form in the billows. How small, how speechlessly she herself had stood beside that other, yonder by the oak! What a homely little flower was she herself beside that splendid exotic! With what spirit, with what fire that other one could speak—and how shyly she herself brought out such every-day words. Was it a marvel, that the poet turned away from her and followed the admired singer? But even if she were not beautiful, not proud, not intellectual, she yet had a sense of her own worth, and would not allow herself to be insulted with impunity.

Come ye waves, and if ye have kissed the dark hair of the bathing beauty, then rush upon the strand and efface for evermore the name of the poet, which, with the point of a parasol, love has written upon the sand; efface it there, and also—in my heart.

Scalding tears gushed from the maiden's eyes, she shut the window that the surging of the distant sea might not reverberate in her dreams like a triumphal song of victorious love! Weeping, she threw herself upon her bed, but then slept soundly and well, as youth can sleep.

She owned a determined mind, she had indeed cast clods of earth upon the coffin of a first, tender affection, which, as yet, had hardly outgrown the incipient bud.

CHAPTER II.

THE BLUE CAMPANULA.

Woodland gloom—high beeches form a temple's hall—mighty oaks keep watch before it; in their midst a green glade in which a hill rises clad with weeping willows and large fronded ferns growing on every side.

Eva sits upon the hill, she has fled from the forester's little house, whither the party of visitors from Warnicken had made an excursion, which was presided over by the Regierungsrath, who knew all the paths in these beautiful Samland woods. There was the Frau Gerichtsräthin with her daughters, the Frau Banquier with her gallant son, whose Latin mistakes made him uncertain of the upper form in the Kniephof College, but who had a flower culled from a poetical casket ready for every lady; there were yet other ladies and girls all in light straw hats, beneath which the withered faces of town cousins looked very odd; yet they, too, all continued their handicraft here, and the echoes of the woods and the little room of the forest-house rang again with city tales, and with the recapitulation of every folly that occurred in the town of pure reason.

Eva fled from this sociable circle; alone she followed a footpath into the wood, farther and farther until she reached that solitude, that spot dedicated to melancholy, where the weeping willows rock whisperingly in the wind.

There she gathered rosemary, and, like Ophelia, began to deck herself with it; she thought of her buried love, and her whole former life seemed so sad to her, so worthy of tears! Her mother's picture, who weeping had once left her, rose before her, for the Frau Räthin was not her mother, the Kalzows were her adopted parents, who never spoke of her real mother, never! No token of the latter's existence ever reached the daughter; she must tarry in some far-off place, must have to suffer, to atone for something; never was her name mentioned in society, and little Eva, herself, for eight years, had been Fräulein Kalzow in the eyes of God and man, and this had all been carried out correctly, and according to the universal law of the country as the Regierungsrath always said, when he wished to denote that anything was particularly excellent and admirable.

But Eva still saw her mother before her! it was indeed a touching picture; the pale lady with those large, enthusiastic eyes, which the daughter had inherited; for the small, sparkling coal black eyes of her adopted mother had nothing in common with that heritage, and she saw these orbs veiled in tears, as she had seen them at the last farewell, and thus this picture accompanied her through life.

And again the weeping willows rustled! How gloomy was the boarding school, were the classes! Eva was no light-hearted girl, and was avoided by the other pupils; questions were upon her lips that did not stand in the catechism, nor in her school books; these queries displeased her teachers, all the more so, because often they could not give an answer to the enquiries; the best meaning one amongst the governesses jokingly called Eva the little philosopher; but in the school she was universally called the girl with the inquiring eyes. Her eyes did indeed speak many questions of her heart to which life alone could impart a reply. Yet Eva was not happy! Her heart thirsted after love; but she did not possess the art of winning it easily by ready acquiescence.

Once, it might be in her twelfth year, she had found a little friend, an innocent girl with merry eyes, who attached herself to Eva like a burr. The latter even became merry in her company, beginning to jest, to play, to dance with the child. This continued throughout one whole winter; when the little one returned after the Easter holidays, she was distant and shy towards Eva, and withdrew entirely from her. For long Eva bore this unmerited estrangement silently, at last she enquired its cause.

"I am not to associate with you," replied the little one, with downcast eyes, "on account of your mother—"

This word buried itself deeply in the girl's heart, and became united to all her sad thoughts; and again in the head class of the school, an enlightened teacher, who in deep draughts had inhaled the air of pure reason which was wafted thither from the Königsberg philosophical dyke, had made remarks about the sad consequences of false piety, which could be seen in many near examples, and thereupon all her schoolfellows looked with meaning glances at Eva, who became alarmed at the enigmatic nature of this insinuation.

Thus she had a right to enquire with her eyes, and with her heart; because a dark shadow fell upon her life.

And again the weeping willows rustled! should no friend then approach her, no love adorn her life? The only one of whom she had dreamed that he might stand nearer to her heart, had become estranged from her again, and her life was lonelier than ever!

But why the wreath of rosemary? Does he deserve such mourning, who flutters heedlessly from flower to flower? No, he does not deserve it. And she flung the rosemary wreath aside; she left the shade of the weeping willows and through the high, bushy ferns sprang down the hill.

"A blue campanula the proud singer called me; good, so may they ring around me, those blue bells; I will be sad no more, I will deck myself with the joyous, open hearted children of the wood."

And she hastened into the cooler valley where the woodland rivulet rippled between alders, and plucked the tiny bells of the wood, the flower of the manifold campanula, which like a blue ribbon intersected the valley.

"I will be glad," murmured she to herself, as, sitting upon the moss-clad roots in the shade of a wide-spreading oak, she twined the large flowered bells into a wreath for her head, while she twisted the smaller ones into a garland, and thus she adorned herself like a wood nymph. The green blooming girdle set off her slender form to advantage.

And she began to sing a cheerful song, as though she would take her own joyful mood by surprise.

Suddenly there arose a rustling in the bushes, and a man in shooting dress stood before her. She sprang up in alarm, then stood still in confusion, and cast her eyes to the ground.

"I regret that I should disturb you," said the stranger, "but I felt constrained to satisfy myself as to whence came such lovely singing."

"The wood belongs to all the world," replied she, "and above all to sportsmen."

"Like yourself, my Fräulein, I am merely a visitor here, I certainly have a right to disturb the stags and hinds, which at such a season of the year have no claims to be spared, but on no account may I startle other living creatures out of lovely hiding places."

Eva now raised her eyes, and regarded the stranger with a cursory glance; his figure was tall and slight, his features seemed to be bronzed by a southern sun, his eyes were half closed, listlessness lay in their glance, but a gentle, refined smile played upon his lips.

"I did not expect to find so charming a flower-fairy in this extensive forest, where the hart-royals dwell. You are as completely buried beneath leaf and flowers, as a Chinese woman of the wood, because if these little bells could ring, they would yield a far sweeter peal than that which the women of the Celestial Empire tinkle before their ancestors' images."

"Have you heard those bells ring?" asked Eva, with that boldness, which is often merely an indication of great embarrassment.

"Certainly, my beautiful fairy! I have heard the bells of human folly in

14

every zone; they have much the same sound in all parts; one flies from them, and finds them again everywhere; however, why should one destroy this charming woodland quiet with such thoughts? But yet. Robbers everywhere! Do not be alarmed my lovely child! I am not one of them, I only mean the hawks which hover yonder about the summits! The nightingales have already winged their southern flight, it is a pity! Their songs would sound so exquisitely here in the valley as an accompaniment to a living picture, to this *fleur animée*, the lovely *campanula*!"

Again Eva ventured to raise her glance, and saw a wide-open blue eye resting upon her. She had been mistaken before, when she deemed it to be small and insignificant; she thereupon recollected that there are eyes upon which the lids rest with heavy pressure, then suddenly seem to shake off this weight and gleam with a full, bright light.

"I am ashamed of myself," said she, already more confidentially, "it was childish folly to deck myself with these flowers. I was sitting over there upon the hill beneath the weeping willows, you probably know the little spot. Suddenly, my heart became filled with fear, I hastened down into the valley, and fancied I should become more cheerful, if all these flowers' eyes looked at me when placed quite close beside me."

"Still so young and yet sad?" asked the stranger, as he drew nearer concernedly, removing his fowling piece from his shoulder, and leaning upon it.

"Nor do I myself know why," replied Eva with embarrassment, "it seems to be wafted over us! There is indeed so much sadness in the world."

"Yet if it does hover about in the air, it only settles and remains there where personal experience makes one susceptible of it, and what can a young girl have experienced?"

"Little and much!"

"You speak as if you were a sybil, promulgating mysterious prophecies!"

"Ah, no, my Herr! Little that can be told, what is but little for others, but unutterably much for myself!"

"Then no bankrupt father, no dead mother, no brother fallen in a duel?"

"Nothing of that kind!"

"Perhaps even a school friend, who, married before—"

"Oh, how you scoff!"

"Or, perhaps a dear friend, who has transferred his heart to another's

15

keeping!"

Eva became red, and looked down upon the ground; the sportsman struck his gun against the earth.

"Oh, that I could leave it alone! You are right; this scoffing tone is horrid. Yet it is a means of defence against the world, and those who have learned to know it, at home and abroad, use it, and it becomes a habit to them; but here, where such sweetly-charming innocence encounters me in the shadow of the tall forest trees, here I might adopt another tone, as I feel my heart also is quite different. Truly, I feel as if in a fairy tale! If there were still enchanted princesses, I should believe I had found one here, and I am already looking round for the monster that guards you, so that in knightly combat I may release you from the dragon; I have an incomparable weapon; my bullet will penetrate through any scaly armour."

"But we are talking too long, my Herr," said Eva, rising. "Excuse me, but my friends are expecting me."

"Then, of course, I must retire," replied the sportsman, as he stepped respectfully on one side.

Eva bowed pleasantly, and followed the path which led into the valley.

"May I ask, my Fräulein, where you wish to go?" said the stranger's voice, behind her; "on this road you would go still farther into the forest! That, indeed, confirms my idea that you dwell in some invisible fairy-palace, as queen of this wood, or that you are, after all, only a flower-spirit, that will float away to dance in the air with elves."

"I am, indeed, quite confused," said Eva, turning back. "Yonder lies the hill, with the weeping willows, and yet I hardly even know by which road I reached it! My friends will be seeking me; they will be uneasy about me! The sun already begins to glow with evening's red, between the tree-stems from the west, instead of beaming above their heads."

"If you really belong to mortal beings, my Fräulein, and even to the most prosaic class of them, who are known under the name of seaside visitors—"

"Now you are right, my Herr!"

"And if you will initiate me into the secret of the point whence you commenced this solitary wandering in the wood, I will guide you to the right road."

Eva told the name of the forest-house where her friends were resting.

"Then you must confide yourself to my unwelcome companionship."

"I am grateful to you, my Herr!"

"Oh, is it not a little adventure for you to wander through this wilderness, accompanied by a gentleman, who happily no longer can be accounted a young one. I certainly have experienced adventures enough in teak and palm groves, with tigers and crocodiles, and have wandered through forests with brown and black beauties, while apes and parrots looked on enviously; but to tell the truth, this nice little adventure in the Royal Prussian chase has a greater charm for me than the encounters with beauties who shine in native brown like old mahogany."

They were now passing by the hill. The heather, which grew wild upon it, was bathed in the evening's crimson, which also flooded the quivering bowed branches of the weeping willows.

Eva did not take any notice of it; she was quite absorbed in her conversation with the stranger.

"Oh, you cannot think, my Fräulein, how a man's mind develops, not only with his wider aims, but also with his more extensive travels. So much weighed upon me; my fatherland had grown too small for me; I was a dreamer and an enthusiast; and as such, had laden myself with guilt."

"It pleases you, doubtlessly, to accuse yourself," said Eva. "Those are generally the best people who perceive so many dark spots in their own life."

"Did your governess tell you that?" said the sportsman, smiling. "The good lady may be mistaken."

"How disagreeable you are," said Eva, petulantly.

"Believe me, it was bad enough! Even now, when I feel myself freer, I often see the old shadow cross my path. But in those days the world's contempt pursued me in such a manner as to crush me to the ground. Only when I convinced myself that the world, as it is called, is merely a very small, fading portion of the great world through which I wandered, that what is whispered and insinuated here on the East Sea, becomes of no importance already on the Adriatic, and still less so far, far away on the Pacific, since then I became storm-proof and invulnerable to the little pin-pricks of public opinion, to the gossip of the provincial neighbourhood. But what am I telling you! You do not yet know what all this means, and that you do not know it, that I can see how strange the dark legend of human guilt is to you, that it is which refreshes and benefits me so intensely. You still possess a delicate little conscience that at the outside ticks like a watch; my own alarms me with the groaning beats of a large clock, such as that which hangs at the Kremlin in Moscow."

"If you were in earnest about it," replied Eva, "you would not pass it over in such a light tone."

"Life, thought, feeling, my Fräulein, with you are all cast in one mould. Therefore, you do not comprehend how, in a man of the world, it is all in confusion, how often in him his soul weeps, while his thoughts spend themselves in frivolous raillery."

"That is a bad habit," said Eva. "Why do people turn everything topsy-turvy? Nature must run its course; the tree with its straight growth strives to attain the summit, the plant the blossom, and both Heaven! What, then, would our good Lord say to His world if the trees wished suddenly to stand upon their heads, stirred up the earth with them, and with their roots sought to reach the sky?"

"There are plants, though, my Fräulein, which one can turn upside down, and which then continue to grow briskly; perhaps I am some kind of offshoot of that species. Yet, seriously speaking, my Fräulein, we stand immeasurably higher than Nature, and, therefore, can fall immeasurably lower."

Eva seemed to be lost in meditation, when she heard her companions' voices, calling her name, sound through the aisles of beeches.

"We are at our goal," said the sportsman, "a few more steps and at a turn of the road you will see the roof of the forester's lodge."

"I thank you, my Herr!"

"But you shall not escape me thus! You penetrated much too far into the Royal Forest; I am a sort of assistant to the chief Forester, and must enquire about your antecedents. If I have understood the echo of these beech-aisles correctly, your name reminds one of Paradise, and it shall also remind me of it."

"I am called Eva, my Herr."

"Yet we no longer live in those primitive days when a Christian name sufficed to prove our identity before the Creator and created."

"My name is Eva Kalzow!"

"And your father?"

"Regierungsrath."

"How prosaic! One meets a fairy in the wood, and her father is a Regierungsrath! And now, you live—"

"In Warnicken, my Herr!"

"Thank you; the enquiry is closed, so far as I am concerned. I am an official personage, who has neither the duty nor the right to introduce himself by name. Think that I am the wild huntsman who traverses the woods at night with black hounds and halloes, but by day escorts lovely women. I shall not, however, place the campanula in my herbarium, but in a vase of fresh water, where bouquets of sweet recollections bloom. Farewell, my Fräulein!"

The stranger took leave with a courteous inclination.

Eva's glances followed him into the thicket, while the Kanzleiräthin, with her round, buxom daughter drew near from the other side.

"You were surely not alone, Eva?" said the latter. "I heard the bushes rustle over there."

"And how we have sought you; it is late already," remarked the Kanzleiräthin, as she put on her spectacles, in order to examine the girl from head to foot and see whether some adventure did not peep out of the folds of her dress.

"I had lost my way," said Eva, "and had fallen asleep beneath the weeping willows! There I dreamed of a wild huntsman; he took me upon his steed, and we sped through the air like a whirlwind."

"Eva, where are you?" resounded the Regierungsrath's voice. "The mists are beginning to rise from the marshes; we shall take cold on our way home."

"I have seen the Erl-king, papa, with the golden hoop; yet I am still alive, and you will take me home safe and sound, and not as a dying child."

And, beginning to warble Schubert's song of the Erl-King, Eva walked on with firm steps and exalted demeanour, in front of the home-bound party.

CHAPTER III.

DUAL LOVE AND EVIL REPUTE.

A few days later, two strangers engaged in eager conversation sat together in the garden-square, between the four Kur-houses of Bad Neukuhren. In the one, notwithstanding that he wore fashionable summer garments, we again recognise the sportsman of the forest, whose sun-burnt features contrasted so strongly with the light straw hat and light-coloured clothes; the other gazed morosely from beneath an untidy felt hat, his sharp furrowed face, which was, however, cast in a noble and somewhat elevated mould, suited the muscular figure.

He might have been taken for a sailor, owing to the power and determination that lay in his whole appearance, had not a refined spiritual expression in his eyes shown that he was wont to occupy himself with intellectual subjects.

"I rejoice, dear Doctor, to have become better acquainted with you here," said the sportsman, "the companions of my own position are somewhat too coolly indifferent to everything that interests me. At the Chief Forester's, things are conducted too patriarchally, and, therefore, I fled to the sea to distract my mind. I will only return to my castle when the rebuilding of the one wing is completed. I gave the architect the exact plan; but always to be present oneself, and to watch its being carried out, is not in accordance with my taste. Everything unfinished is odious to me; those lime pits, those carts of stone, those scaffoldings, make an uncomfortable impression upon me. Therefore, I accepted the Chief Forester's invitation at first, he being an old friend of my father."

"How long have you been back in Europe, Herr Von Blanden?" asked the Doctor.

"I have been in Europe for two years; but during that time I have exhausted the romance of the south; spent two summers on the Italian lakes, whose charms are indescribable! I have seen the Highland lakes in the giant mountains of Thibet and the sun of Palestine; yet the peculiarity of a Lago Maggiore; that balminess that hovers over the water, the islands, the shores, cannot be found elsewhere! My father's death, two month's ago, recalled me to East Prussia; it marked a turning point in my life."

"You became rich," said the Doctor.

"I have never needed to trouble myself about money, and I consider that a great advantage. Those are unhappy mortals who, amongst all the other ills of life, must also take that vile metal into consideration in everything that they do or wish! Is there a more inconsolable slavery than that of dependance upon money? Therein consists the happiness of riches, that they do not know these limits."

"The German student does not know them either," interposed the Doctor, "or, rather, will not know them. Youth is free! But the unpaid accounts follow us for many long years, and a frowning father reminds us that this youthful freedom belongs to the kingdom of dreams."

"Thus, it was not that," continued Blanden, "which made such a metamorphosis in my life; yet I returned with the firm determination to put an end, at last, to the epoch of adventures by land and sea; not to seek an object in life in the refined, inordinate longing after enjoyment of travelling; not in the varying circumstances which it offers to the mind and heart, but rather in active, earnest work, and, above all, by these means, to extinguish the unpleasant recollections that cling to my past."

"Youthful recollections!" said the Doctor, as he removed his felt hat, and took advantage of its pliability to press it into diverse forms, "who has not similar ones to note down in his diaries? And, after all, one may ask if these wanderings astray do not give more worth to life, than our exertions drawn by rule and measure?"

"But, at some time, one must put an end to it, I feel that! Far abroad as one may have wandered, a man must sometime prove to his nearest, his relations, his country associates that he has changed, that he can do something, can work, that he can do his duty to his neighbour, although he may see farther than they all."

"It does not require much to do that," said the Doctor, as he pushed his somewhat tangled hair from his forehead. "Our landed gentry's horizon does not extend far beyond the price of corn in summer, beyond *l'ombre* and sleighing parties in the winter. Here they possess a peculiar instrument called a *zoche*, with which they attack Mother Earth's body! All the world uses the plough; here they have the *zoche*, a two-legged agricultural implement of very ancient date! This *zoche* is a species of East Prussian symbol; we do not imitate it, but that which we possess ourselves is still less worthy of imitation."

"I must defend my brother squires, best of Doctors," replied Von Blanden, "there are many sterling, educated men amongst them, and especially amongst those whom I must still reckon as my opponents, to gain whose friendship is a wish very dear to my heart. Yes, dear Doctor," continued von Blanden, "I am contented with the spirit which now pervades this province, and the conditions are favourable to my plan. Here we have a public life, which, until now, has been wanting; the political spirit is awakened, and, if it was always painful for me, in the midst of the life and bustle of London and Paris, where great political questions stirred all minds, to think of the intensely quiet home and its inhabitants, who, like political backwoodsmen, live in the densest gloom of ignorance and indifference, now a joyous feeling fills me at the thought that the first pulse's throbs of constitutional existence are heard here, that all Germany gazes at the Baltic shores, at our East Prussia."

The Doctor shook his head.

"It may be, may be! It is a little better than formerly; but all politics are merely a struggle about forms! No one becomes happier by them. A more deeply penetrating revolution is necessary. The old views of the world must change their grooves."

"Those were the dreams of my youth! I longed for a new religion, which should develop itself out of the old one; yet one learns gradually to limit oneself to the Possible. You are still a young man; I am thirty-six years old; a decade lies between us! At that age I was an enthusiast like you! Now, I look upon the groundwork of political liberty as the most worthy object to strive for, by means of which we first become the equals of other nations. My wishes are to be elected to the Provincial Diet. A general representation will not long have to be waited for. I will pledge my mental power, the whole of my experiences upon it."

"Always practical!" muttered the Doctor to himself, "and, at the same time, it is nothing but misty theory! The Provincial Diet to be united to the General Diet—possible! Perhaps some day, too, we may even have a Parliament. Many grand discourses will be held there; but so long as Government holds the reins in its hands, it will do as it chooses, let others speak as they may."

"I do not look so gloomily upon matters," said Blanden. "The world's spirit becomes elevated by a more liberal organisation. I long for political labour, but shall not for it neglect the management of my estate. I have learnt much abroad, and also look upon the world from the position of a landowner. And then—if a man will do anything great in a narrow circle, he must limit himself in every respect, form a domestic hearth, and, in fact, I am resolved to marry!"

"The Philistines are upon you, Sampson!" cried the Doctor, as he crushed his hat angrily on to his head.

"What is there so astounding in it?" asked Blanden.

Now the Doctor was riding his favourite hobby!

"Marry! The thought makes my blood boil!"

"Then you are easily excited. What all the world does—"

"Is exactly that which one must not do," interrupted the Doctor.

"There we have the *zoche*, instead of the plough!" said Blanden, smiling.

"No, respected friend! I am a practical doctor, although until now I may only have cured few sick; but in the same illnesses I should not prescribe the same remedies to all constitutions. Natures such as ours are not fitted for matrimony. For it, steady, equable minds are needed—we do not possess them. Any one who is accustomed to a variety of sensations would be killed by everlasting sameness. Marriage cannot be happy without blinkers; but is it happiness to wander through life in them?"

"Alas, you are an incorrigible radical, who attacks everything!"

"A man must study himself!" said the Doctor, as he assumed a tone of instruction. "He must study the original phenomenon, and that is his own heart. After observing myself closely, I cannot but believe that marriage in general is no beneficent arrangement; at least it is not for such natures as mine. It is based upon the dogma of one faith which alone can bring salvation; it requires of the husband, 'You shall have none other gods but me!' But I could not confine myself to this love; I consider this exclusiveness of affection to be one of the greatest drawbacks with which mankind has been indoctrinated, not only by its priests, but also by its great poets with their tragedies of love and jealousy. Not alone for Turkish sensuality, but for the most intellectual and imaginative view of life, such exclusiveness is an obstructive barrier! And what narrow-mindedness lies in this wilful possession, which feels hatred and enmity towards everything, and lays claim to the same right! How indeed can any one talk of rights, when free affection is in question? Why should not two women love the same man, and be loved by him, without wishing to tear each other into pieces? Is it not more natural and more human that similar emotions and affections should dwell together in peace? I know that this is boundless heresy, and yet it is my conviction. Richly endowed natures which would live their lives cannot exhaust their hearts in one single love."

"Halt, halt," Blanden smilingly interrupted the eccentric Doctor, "You cannot thus, with one breath, cast existing customs to the winds."

Doctor Kuhl did not feel himself beaten; he pushed his chair uneasily back and forward, sprang up, and with arms folded, defiantly continued to force his worldly wisdom upon his companion. Kuhl was known along the shores of the Baltic Sea by his Herculean strength. He was a preserver of life by profession; wherever misfortunes loomed, he was present. He caught the reins of runaway horses; where any one was, voluntarily or involuntarily, near death in the water, Doctor Kuhl appeared as a guardian angel. He was an excellent swimmer, and when the flag hung out in the sea-baths, forbidding people to bathe because a storm stirred up the billows of the East Sea, Doctor Kuhl was sure to hazard a conflict with the waves, as the only living creature who at once defied the tempest and bathing-police. By means of all these valiant deeds, he had become more popular than any other person, and even in society his extreme views, of which he made no secret, were pardoned. He was simply considered eccentric, and public opinion judged him by an exceptional standard.

"Look here, dear fellow," he continued his lecture, "you know both the Fräulein von Dornau, Olga and Cäcilie; may heaven's and their mother's anger punish me! I love them both at once, and with the finest apothecary's scales could not discover the least preponderance of either in the balance."

"And what, then, do these ladies say to your simultaneous love?"

"I believe I have already somewhat converted them to my theory, even although the old Adam or the old Eve in them still rebels against it. On days so full of vigour as this, when the ocean glistens in the sunshine, and a fresh breeze blows hither from the north, when the feeling of strength fills my breast, then Olga is my calendar's saint. She possesses something fresh, natural, voluptuous in all her being, something Juno-like, and even the large eye is not wanting, which old Homer eulogises with such a base comparison. I will not say for a moment that a large mind speaks from that large eye, but Nature has made everything abundant about her. She reminds me of hotels, in which everything is arranged with the greatest comfort; nor must large plate glass windows be wanting there, either."

"That is, indeed," interposed Blanden, "quite a new form of praise of the fair sex, and our poets might go to school to you."

"She is purely sensual life," continued the Doctor, without letting himself be disturbed by this interlocutory remark. "All nature, instinct, little knowledge, no reason; she does not raise any special opposition even to my most daring views. It is quite different with Cäcilie: she is my calendar's saint for intellectual days; she is slighter, more refined; she has something

24

Lacertian about her, that escapes one easily, that one would always grasp anew; everything about her has form, body and mind. She argues with me, she refutes, her eyes scintillate, and yet in the midst of the conflict she seems suddenly to lay down her arms; if her delicate lips do weave the most ingenious arguments wherewith to conquer me, the charm of submission lies already in her eyes. She is a Penelope; her mind weaves a web, that her heart ever again unravels. Olga acts by the charm of nature's body, Cäcilie by the charm of the spirit. I bear both in my heart; I stand as closely to the one as to the other. Shall I sacrifice one part of my being, in order to do homage to exclusive love?"

"We have," said Blanden, "no social forms in which a dual love could be lastingly secured; it is indeed a daring, yes, reprehensible innovation."

"Not at all," replied the Doctor. "It is the greatest secret of our society but certainly is only seldom spoken of; yet sometimes when you open books of the history of literature, in the lives of gifted men, you will find pages on which it is legibly written! Think of Bürger, of Doris and Molly; think of Schiller, of Charlotte and Caroline. How candid are the confessions of our great poets! I do not flatter myself I am the first who makes this great discovery, but I utter it fearlessly; this is Nature's law, which society outlaws, while it exercises its secret dominion undisturbedly."

"That may hold good during the stormy impetuous period of life," said Blanden. "I have experienced it in every quarter of the globe. Now I long for tranquillity, for restriction; I know that now in it alone can I find happiness, and I have no longing to lead either an Olga or a Cäcilie home, but a sweet, modest maiden who has not yet developed into independent womanliness, who is still capable of being formed, and growing up to twine herself around me."

"The old fable," replied Doctor Kuhl, scoffingly; "as if ever a girl was formed or changed by a man! Girls are the pure elementary spirits, but what they are, they are from the beginning. An elf will never become a nymph, and if one lives in the water and has a fish's tail, no power in the world will make her into a salamander with a sparkling golden crown."

"All the same," said Blanden, "I shall take an elf, and be satisfied with it."

"Then you have probably already found the one beauty which can make you happy?" asked the Doctor, inquisitively.

"Indeed, I almost think it," replied Blanden. "Lately, in the forest, I made the acquaintance of a beautiful wood-maiden, and I shall soon renew it in Warnicken."

"Well, you have my blessing," said the Doctor, with annoyance, crushing the felt hat, which in the meantime had again become a plaything in his hands, violently on to his head.

At this moment, the pair of sisters walked past the friends; Olga and Cäcilie came out of the sea, and, as is customary at bathing places, let their long wet, nymph-like hair flow down to dry in the sun. They both had splendid figures; the one fuller, the other slighter.

The Doctor greeted them with an eager bow, and soon found himself sailing in the wake of the elder sister, while the younger one, with a slight side movement sent a whole broadside of fiery glances upon him.

Blanden meditated over the peculiarity of those singular fellows who seek to bring everything into a system, of which they at last become the slaves. A hand was suddenly placed upon his shoulder, and his neighbour, Freiherr von Wegen, looked at him good-temperedly, as he turned round—

"There, I have found you at last; I sought you in vain at the Chief Forester's."

"Well, and what news do you bring me?" Blanden asked the fair, affectionate friend of his childish and youthful days, who, since his return, had become his indispensable assistant.

Wegen took a chair, lighted his cigar, beckoned to the waiter, and then began in an important manner—

"It is fatal, really fatal!"

"What then?" asked Blanden.

"That stupid story of former days!"

"Well."

"You know that I travel about as your agent, from estate to estate, in order to ensure your election to the Diet, and I am a commercial traveller who is not afraid of being seen. I advance all your qualifications—first-rate recommendations, clever, great traveller, wealthy, undoubted possessions! So far I met with no dispute. Liberal—then the symptoms of questioning begin. 'Liberal?' says Oberamtmann von Schlöhitten, whom I sought in his sheep-fold, while he examined his breed of sheep, one of the few which can exist in Silesia and Australia—'well as yet he has given no proof of it.' 'Only first elect him, and the proofs will follow,' replied I, prompt to serve. 'Now, from what I know about it—he belonged to the religious set—that is a species which I cannot endure, wolves in sheep's clothing!' He had by this time arrived at the principal ewe, whose fleece he allowed to glide through his fingers with satisfaction. I utilised this moment of tranquil delight, and said —'That was in his youth, he has changed.' 'Any one who changes his colours so quickly,' said the Oberamtmann, disagreeably, as he released the mother sheep with a loud smack, 'is not fitted for a representative! They stand bold to their colours!'"

"Well," said Blanden, "we will generously relinquish that vote."

"Yes, if it were the only one! I went to the wealthy Milbe of Kuhlwangen, the same who once announced in the newspapers; always of Kuhlwangen, but seldom in Kuhlwangen—that man is every inch a peasant, but he is a splendid humorist; he was just looking at a horse, that had arrived fresh from Trakehner; I went straight to my point. 'Blanden,' asked he, 'is that the same Blanden who was mixed up in that ugly Königsberg affair?' 'That was ten years ago,' replied I. 'That is all the same, the mark has been burnt into him like this Trakehner stud-brand.' He also invited me to a good breakfast, that I enjoyed thoroughly, although it was not without reluctance that I broke bread and drank wine at the table of a man who turned so deaf an ear to my proposals."

"Dear friend," said Blanden, "in politics one must accustom oneself to failure."

"But not when it comes thick as hail," replied Wegen, as he struck the table with his riding-whip, and with his left hand angrily curled his fair moustache. "There was Hermann von Gutsköhnen, Sengern von Laerchen, they only knew that you are a large and rich landed proprietor, and will give you their votes; there they live upon their sixty acres, and plough their manors themselves; they are homely people who understand nothing of the world."

"Now I know, according to your views, where I must seek my supporters."

"Graf von Donahoff," Wegen continued his report, "received me very pleasantly; he belongs to those nobles, about whose party-leaning I was still uncertain; he is connected with the Liberals by marriage. 'Blanden,' cried he, 'surely a pious man, one of those who remained true to his creed and defied calumny; we Conservatives should have a good supporter in him!' I hardly dared to undeceive the man with silvery locks. And yet it must be done! 'A Liberal, then?' exclaimed he, 'that is inconsolable! If that species now grows wild here in our province, well so be it; but when men who have drank at our refreshing well of salvation, are so fickle as to go over to the camp of the unrighteous, one could shed burning tears!' And he folded his hands, yet what was worse, he poured me out no more of that exquisite Madeira which stood upon the table; for he had discovered that I, too, wandered upon the paths of the godless, and sat amongst the seats of the scornful; I took leave very dejectedly, and disappeared as though the earth had swallowed me up."

"Oh, I know—a sister of his formerly belonged to our sect; she, too, in the meanwhile has become a Liberal, since she married, and has seceded disgracefully."

"Yes, the women, dear Blanden," said Wegen, shrugging his shoulders, "the women, you are really in their black books! Baron von Fuchs is a very sensible man, he recognises your mental superiority, is ready to give you his vote, and has only a smile for the reproaches which are brought against you on all sides. He invited me to dinner. I took my place triumphantly beside the lady of the house, who helped me liberally. We had just arrived at the joint— no, it was at the pudding—now I recollect it quite accurately, when the conversation turned upon you. 'Only to name such a man,' cried the Baroness, angrily, and threw her knife and fork upon the table. I received no more of the delicious wine-sauce. 'Well, what more is there?' said the Baron, as with great equanimity he poured himself out a glass of Johannisberger, 'we are going to return him to the Assembly!' Then the storm broke loose. 'That wicked man, that hypocrite—no Adalbert, if you do that!—I do not trouble myself about your politics, I never have troubled myself about them; but if you make your Assembly into a Sodom and Gomorrah, all we must protest who have been brought up with proper principles, and who know what morality demands! You at least shall not give your vote to Blanden!' and she sprang up from the table, the tart did not go round again, the most beautiful dessert remained untouched. The Baron, as far as appearances went, did not allow himself to be disturbed, but yet he was put out, and I am convinced that she will conquer in this domestic war, because she is a woman of principle—and the devil must manage all such as her."

"Our prospects seem bad," said Blanden, after a pause, while he sat lost in meditation, "I shall feel it most painfully if my new wish to take to active life should meet with insurmountable obstacles, just because I feel the power within me to enter upon new paths, because I have the earnest desire to break with my past, because I would as it were grasp the firm shore, I should not like to be hurled back into the breakers."

"Dear friend," replied Baron von Wegen, "all is not lost as yet! The Landrath is on your side, and he commands a considerable number of electors, but you must take decided steps yourself."

"And which?" asked Blanden.

"You must return to your castle; the rebuilding of the one wing will be ready in a few days; you must pay visits yourself amongst your neighbours; you are a kindly fellow at heart—and that after all is the principal thing; before it all the *on dit* disappear, what people say and what they think! Then invite them all to a sumptuous dinner, and they will come, be convinced! You are still one of the most respected landowners, whom they will not dare to scorn. But a good dinner opens people's hearts, I know it! When once the *veuve Cliquot* is uncorked, and she exercises her magical influence, then people allow themselves to be persuaded to anything, to which otherwise they do not show the slightest inclination. Then you can hold a little electioneering speech. You are a master of oratory, and you will see, even those obstinate von Schlöhitten and Kuhlwangen will pledge themselves to follow your standard. A good dinner is not only the most agreeable thing that there is—but also under certain circumstances the most necessary! I know it!"

"You may be right, dear Caspar—"

"For heaven's sake do not address me by my Christian name, I hate it! I always think of the Free-shooter and the 'Wolf's schlucht,' when I hear myself spoken to by it, or what is still much worse, of the 'Kasperle Theatre.'"

"But before I go home, I must take three or four days more leave."

"What for?"

"I wish to go across to Warnicken; I have discovered a treasure there, that I must inspect more closely; perhaps I shall adorn my castle with it."

"Good heavens—a love adventure!" said Wegen, humming—

> 'Reich mir die hand mein Leben!
> Komm 'auf mein Schloss mit mir!'

"Always the same old Don Juan!"

"You are mistaken! The marble governor took him away long ago! It is a more serious love affair, but which, I allow, requires careful scrutiny."

"Indeed," said Wegen, while his good-natured face assumed a peculiarly kindly expression. "Marriage would not be the most stupid of all the things that you have done hitherto. A married man—that sounds so respectable, inspires such confidence! I have always thought that it would be a most fortunate move on the board. The queen would then rule over all the squares! Everything in the past is forgiven and forgotten! If an amiable young woman is not alarmed at that past, then all will probably follow her example, and even the Baroness von Fuchs will beat the retreat. I do not care much for matrimony, I shall remain a bachelor. A *fiancée* may be an angel, but one never knows how she may cook when she is one's wife. And a constantly bad *cuisine*—I should prefer the infernal regions!"

"You encourage me, old friend; it pleases me! Then—leave for four days! Perhaps they will be the most important in my life—and after that, back to the Castle!"

"I will ride over to my place to-day, and will see that things are right on yours."

"Thank you! And afterwards I will invite a newly-made friend to stay with me—Doctor Kuhl—he is an original fellow; but I like people to have and express new ideas."

"Then I am not sufficient for you, dear friend!" replied Wegen, stroking his blonde moustache in a melancholy manner. "Certainly, I possess few new ideas! Only at a good dinner they pour in upon me; then I understand what the poets call inspiration—I am often astonished at myself."

"You are good-natured," said Blanden, pressing his friend's hand, "and that is worth more than all this world's wisdom. Then we will seek Kuhl—he was abducted by two fair women."

"Stop, stop!" cried Wegen, with a pathetic gesture. "I am still breathless with my business-journies and reports, and you would have this state of exhaustion continue still longer? Storm and tempest—we have fasted long enough; now for a substantial breakfast! A few glasses of sherry, to defy wind and weather, and a beefsteak as underdone as possible—in that I am an Englishman!"

He beckoned to a waiter, and tied a napkin, that was lying upon the table, round his neck, brandishing his knife and fork impatiently in the air.

CHAPTER IV.

BATHING-PLACE PICTURES.

The Samland coast is frequented but little by strangers; the list of visitors seldom contains a Russ or Pole. However, a great number of people flows from East Prussia, from distant Masure, and its lonely lakes; from the primeval forests of Lithuania, to these homely seaside places; but more especially, the ancient town Ottokars sends its officials, its professors, its students, its young merchants, to the sea, and the sacred ocean-tide often overhears very learned discourses, which are held across the bathing-rope during the pauses which ensue between each rushing wave.

Everything here possesses the charm of fresh primitiveness; the festive bathing gown, the tasteful, fashionable toilet of Western seaside places are unknown.

Youth, full of the love of enterprise, assembles in Neukuhren; small dance in the evening, an expedition in a *leiter-wagon*, in which numerous families are crowded together, a concert, a performance—everything that with small means gives great enjoyment to eager spirits, is provided here by the leaders of social amusements.

Let us follow Doctor Kuhl, with his two friends, upon their way through the watering place.

The respected elders sit before the Kurhouses, newspapers in their hands, and hold council about the State's welfare. The debate is very keen, as it is a time of political agitation. The little Jewish doctor yonder, a follower of Johann Jacoby, defends the "four questions" against a whole bench of judges and councillors, who are beside themselves that the tiny little man's inexhaustible eloquence does not permit them to put in a word. Their lips quiver, their eyes flash; they have armed replies upon their lips, but all attempts are vain, and at last only the energetic bass voice of a minister of finance succeeds, if not in allaying, at least, in deafening him.

A ladies' club is sitting on the terrace of the Kur-house, in questionable morning-costumes. Even the ladies of a certain age, who in the evening still expect to obtain partners for the dance, and even admirers, have as yet neglected to summon the Graces to their toilet-tables; a portion of them sits there in grandmother-like caps; the charming love-locks that in the evening droop so fascinatingly over their temples, still linger in some place of concealment, and no one can foresee that these garments of sackcloth can develop later into elegant draperies. Everything is so homely, so simple, so nun-like; all the more lively is the conversation. A betrothal, which had taken place on the previous evening, gave cause for plentiful shrugging of shoulders, because the gentleman as yet held no respectable position in life, and the *fiancée*, as several female friends asserted, a very uncertain one.

Hardly was this conversation worn out before Doctor Kuhl, passing by with the two Fräuleins Dornau, offered an inexhaustible topic.

Here all considerations were at an end, and the battle-axes were wielded pitilessly. A widow, of dubious age, but of indubitable inclination to marry again, was reckless enough to take the unlucky victims under her protection, as she hazarded the remark, that one sister was at the same time a chaperon for the other. Both the Fräuleins Dornau slight capacity for playing a chaperon's part was then discussed on all sides with exultant eloquence.

Fortunately, the passers-by did not overhear the verdict of this court of censure, which sought to ostracise them from all good society: they walked along the village street. Tents were set up before the fishermen's cottages, beneath which the bathing nomads had taken up their abode. Here a young girl was reading George Sand's newest romance, or Doctor Schöner's poems, little attractive to a female mind as was the young lyrist's daring suggestion of turning the bells into cannon, naturally for the army of liberty which should blow the world out of its grooves. There a young man without any upper light, was attempting to execute a painting of the Samland Sea; the old gentleman, who, in his shirt-sleeves, gazes out of a narrow window in one of the fishermen's cottages, is a Privy Councillor, who had almost attained to being "his excellency:" and yonder, on the bench, in the arbour, if a little erection of boards merits that poetical name, sat one of the most admired beauties from the capital, her embroidery lying idle on her lap, while she herself gazed with dreamy eyes after the goose-herd who drove the unrenowned sisters of the Capitoline celebrities through the village street.

Doctor Kuhl, with his fair friends, had left the village behind him, and found a retired spot beneath whispering birches close by the surging sea, below in the "hollow way."

No inconvenient watchers disturbed them here at this hour of the day; it was as still in the hot sun as it usually only is on a cool, moonlight night.

"Here by the sacred, briny waves of Homer," cried the Doctor, "by the syrens and nereïdes and all the goddesses of the classical Walpurgis-night, I feel within me some of the blood of the dwellers in Olympus, who allowed themselves to be enchanted by beauty and love whenever the latter met them triumphantly. Poor Paris, who had only an apple for one goddess, instead of for all three at once! Yet all were worthy of the prize, and it was lamentable to grant to two only the second best. We three, dear Olga, my Cäcilie, we three form a beautiful union which the world does not understand how to respect!"

"You must allow yourself to understand, that you only actually love Olga!" remarked Cäcilie.

Doctor Kuhl sprang up indignantly.

"Any one hearing you speak in that manner would believe you to be jealous. Jealousy—that fruit of an odious narrow-mindedness, this inculcated social vice, which must always be alien to every natural emotion! Nothing irritates me so much as when I perceive tokens of jealousy in reasonable beings. Jealousy is a natural daughter of envy; but, alas! it has been legitimatised by society."

"On the contrary, dear Paul," replied Cäcilie, "it arises from an inherent feeling which belongs, more or less, to all mankind."

"And if it were so," replied the Doctor in an energetic tone, "one must curb and subdue these inherent feelings by true cultivation. The latter, however, tells us that the human heart is much too rich to exhaust its wealth in one sensation, that, indeed, a man can lay out his feelings, like his capital, in various investments, and that the coupons of the one do not in the remotest degree lose in value because he cuts coupons off the others. You understand me, Olga?"

Olga, who swore blindly by the master's words, nodded her perfect acquiescence, and was rewarded by a kiss for her powers of comprehension; she willingly assented that Doctor Kuhl should cut off this coupon from the invested capital of his feelings.

The sun, rising still higher, however, obliged the three lovers to retire, besides which, Doctor Kuhl had promised a college friend to meet him at the Kur-houses, and therefore he first accompanied the two Fräuleins Dornau to their dwelling, which was situated in a by-street of the village, and was a fisherman's cottage in the word's most daring sense. Mother Dornau, a poor officer's widow, could with difficulty only afford the expenses of a trip to the sea; modest as they might be, she was obliged to stint herself in every respect. Her two daughters' splendid figures could hardly stand uprightly in the two tiny rooms which she had rented there, and were always obliged first to remove out of the way several fishing nets lying upon the threshold when they wished to enter. Frau Rittimeisterin von Dornau, however, hoped to obtain husbands for her daughters by this sea-side visit, as the climate of Neukuhren was particularly favourable to engagements. Therefore she did not hesitate even to break into her small capital for this purpose, so as to cover the outlay of the undertaking. As in addition her hearing was bad and her sight still worse, she could only learn its results from her daughters' reports, and Doctor Kuhl appeared to her to be a very eligible wooer, who at first only seemed to bear a resemblance, which it was to be hoped would soon disappear, to Eulenspiegl's jackass, as it is represented standing between two bundles of hay.

The Doctor, jubilantly humming a song, now went to the Kur-house square, where he had appointed to meet his friend; much to his astonishment, he perceived the latter sitting at a long table, around which were assembled seven young girls and one elderly gentleman in spectacles who appeared to be engaged in some learned discourse, as was clearly evident from the long pauses in his harangue, during which he wiped the glasses of his spectacles, as at the same time he addressed each girl in turn by her Christian name, Doctor Kuhl arrived at the well-founded conclusion that the learned gentleman was the father of these seven daughters, and with the greater reason, because the former's eye rested with satisfaction upon each, much as does the eye of an author upon every single tome of a seven-volumed work. Doctor Kuhl made a sign to his friend; yet the latter did not appear to acknowledge the signal for departure; he only nodded pleasantly, and intimated by plain pantomimic language that for the moment it was impossible for him to follow his friend's hint. Kuhl tried to console himself with a "stiff glass of grog," for he had contracted several sailor-like habits. The elderly gentleman's discourse, in the meantime seemed never to intend to come to an end; several of his daughters could not suppress a sly yawn, and Doctor Reising—that was the young friend's name—pushed his chair impatiently to and fro. At last a conclusion "fast in its prison walls of earth," seemed to comprise the contents of the whole discourse; Doctor Reising rose somewhat impetuously and begged to be excused for a short time; soon the two young friends were seated together, undisturbedly, while the female Round Table cast surreptitious glances across, and examined the new comer's powerfully built figure.

"Who are those seven girls without uniform?" asked Doctor Kuhl, as Reising took a seat beside him.

"My dear fellow," replied the latter, "I am in a peculiar and very difficult position."

"You surely have not to solve a prize problem with the comedy's motto, 'The ugliest of seven?'"

"Do not speak so loudly," said young Doctor Reising, as he looked timidly round at the fair ones. The shyness and timidity of his manner became more apparent as he did so; he was a beardless, fair man, and his blonde hair stood up rather like bristles; his pointed nose seemed somewhat too sharp, and his lean figure was in a state of constant nervous, trembling motion.

"Well, make your confession to me," said Kuhl after a steady pull at the sailor's drink.

"Look here, dear friend," replied Reising, whispering, "you know that I have taken a degree of a Doctor of Philosophy, and contemplate settling down at the university of B—, there a philosopher has the best chance. That gentleman is the most influential Professor of Philosophy in B—, at the same time the only one who reads Logic and Psychology; everything for me, depends upon his favour!"

"I understand," replied Kuhl, "and there are seven charming obstacles."

"You are far from understanding all," said Reising more and more mysteriously; "that Professor is a disciple of Herbart, and I am a follower of Hegel, heart and soul."

"Then I should prefer to go to another University."

"My good friend, my rich uncle, whose heir I expect to be, lives in B—, and he wishes me positively to be near him; I cannot trifle with these prospects. The Hegelite philosophy is not, as it used to be under Altenstein, State's-philosophy which was encouraged, ensuring appointments and posts. A contrary wind blows under Eichhorn's ministry, and I myself incline very much to the wrong side, so I may make use of a rich uncle from whom I have expectations. My thoughts lead me to even bolder results. I require the goodwill of the authorities; but Herbart, I must tell you, my dear friend, it is especially Herbart, who is so unpalatable to me, and much as I would control myself, I cannot do it; I am constantly being drawn into a dispute with Professor Baute; the numberless schools are incomprehensible to me."

"But he seeks to make them more comprehensible by means of his seven daughters."

"That is just the misfortune! I am convinced that I could easily get over the chasm that separates the Hegelite and Herbartian philosophy, if I could resolve to propose to one of his seven daughters; my University career would then be ensured, as certainly as I should receive his daughter's hand; as being my uncle's heir, I am accounted a good match; but my dear friend, I feel nothing as yet!"

"A Hegelite, who would have any feeling!" said Doctor Kuhl, "your master extols marriages of reason! Show in this case, that you are his worthy disciple *hic Rhodus, hic salta!* It is not a question of being in love, and a more rational marriage you can certainly not make."

"And then," whispered Doctor Reising, "if I had mustered the resolution, the choice is so difficult."

"But my dear friend," said Kuhl, "that is quite immaterial. Old Hegel would turn in his grave for joy if you took the first that comes, because it is just as rational to take the one as the other. Count them off on your coat buttons."

"You, like so many others, have misunderstood Hegel," replied Reising, as he assumed an ominous lecturing posture, and placed his finger against his nose.

"Come, now, no college lecture! If you positively must choose, I will help you. Just go through the days of the week and muster these seven saints."

"You are right," whispered Reising, as he passed his hand through his hair, and pushed it up, although it stood rebelliously high enough already, without his doing so. "Do you see the eldest there with the two plaits, that is Euphrasia! She is not good looking, but coquettish! You must allow that those two plaits are only suitable for girls before they are confirmed; the mother was, I believe, a Russian, and now the daughter always coquettes with these two ribbon-interwoven plaits. It looks Panslavistic; I should not wish for Euphrasia at any price."

"Two plaits. You are right," replied Kuhl, laughing, "one is enough for a German professor."

"Ophelia sits beside her!" continued Reising, "she always has something languishing in her glances, in her nature; she is a regular weeping willow! That is not my style! Everything emotional is abhorrent to me!"

"But if you do not take Ophelia," suggested Kuhl, "you will still not get rid of Father Polonius! We will leave Ophelia alone, let her wear the most beautiful wreath in her hair, naturally a willow branch."

"Then follows Emma, that is the little one with the pug-nose. She is not bad, but she has a soul for nothing but cooking, washing, scrubbing, and falls asleep when one addresses a sensible word to her."

"That would not do for a philosopher, who requires an intelligent victim."

"Albertina, that is the biggest one, she has a slight figure, rather too tall, but she is always silent; I have not yet heard her utter three sentences; I might believe that she meditates inwardly upon weighty questions, that she possesses an internal life; but those repulsive, watery blue eyes are so utterly apathetic, I am convinced that she thinks of nothing, and is only silent, because speaking is a labour to her."

"*Si tacuisses!* Yet for a philosopher Albertina is not to be despised; let us make a cross to her name!"

"Beside her sits Lori; she has a pair of sparkling eyes; she is the *enfant terrible*; but such an impudent imp I could not hereafter, as a professor, take into any good society. She scoffs at everything, and is not even witty. Then follow the two youngest, Gretchen and Marie; Gretchen is still like a blank sheet of paper, and Marie even wears short petticoats, and frilled garments."

"Certainly," replied Kuhl. "You cannot wait until the understanding of the one, and the skirts of the other, have grown. Indeed, it is not easy to make a choice here; but who vouches for it that your readings of character are correct! If I should advise you, I must convince myself."

"Very well; then I will introduce you to the Professor, and at the same time to his family."

"In any case my conceptions of these seven girls will then cross the threshold of knowledge with greater facility," replied Kuhl, with an allusion to Herbart's Philosophy, which drew a significant smile from his friend; "but tell me, how does this follower of Herbart come to a Samland bathing place?"

"For one thing, it is a species of pilgrimage to the city of Pure Reason, where Herbart stood so long upon Kant's rostrum, with his blue frock coat, and elegant riding-boots; secondly, he followed a friend's invitation. You, of course, know that worthy Herbartian who always goes to his lectures with a red umbrella, such as the late Lampe, Kant's servant, carried, and looks upon this red umbrella which he places upon a bench, and which gradually transforms itself by some optical delusion into a living being, as the third person, in order to form a college. At present he is bathing; the only student, who is accustomed to listen to him, is also bathing, only the red umbrella is missing; otherwise the college would be complete in the waves of the East Sea."

"You triumph, you Hegelites," replied Kuhl, solemnly; "but the day will come, when even Hegel will be expounded to empty benches:

'When this Imperial Troy

And Priam's race and Priam's royal self
Shall in one common ruin be o'erthrown.'"

Kuhl was soon introduced to Professor Baute and the seven girls. The upholder of polygamy was naturally not in the least degree confused by this female Pleiades. He took advantage of the knowledge which he had already gained as to how the land lay, for very adroit manœuvres by which to win the seven ladies' good-will.

He spoke of the Caucasian beauties' plaits interwoven with pearls with Euphrasia, with Ophelia of the gentle rustle of the weeping birches in the hollow way in the evening's crimson light, with Emma of the worthlessness of the Neukuhren laundresses, especially with respect to shirt fronts; in a short time he was even so successful as to cause Albertina to interrupt her inflexible silence by some silliness, which fully explained her taciturnity; Lori, with great tact, made an allusion to both the Fräuleins Dornau, acknowledged by Doctor Kuhl with a slight bow; Gretchen to say she would learn French, and Marie catch butterflies with him; in short, when the Doctor took leave, all seven voices were unanimous in declaring that he was a most charming man, and Doctor Reising was sadly placed in the shade by him.

The latter perceived this himself, but when he was becoming irritable about it, Kuhl consoled him with saying he should work for his friend in future, so soon as he had discovered the right girl, and established himself firmly in her favour.

Kuhl had hardly risen from table when Blanden, with his friend von Wegen, in a beaming, rosy, wine-flushed mood, went towards him and invited him to come to his Ordensburg in three days' time. Kuhl accepted, and Blanden promised then to recount his adventures in Warnicken, for which place he should set out that night on foot.

Thereupon the Herculean Doctor refreshed himself with a second glass of grog, sprang boldly over several tables that stood in his way, and had soon plunged into the salt waves, which he clove with a powerful arm, while Reising dejectedly bore the costs of the entertainment with the seven possible brides, and, left alone in his glory, played a by no means triumphant part.

CHAPTER V.

THE AMBER MERCHANT.

Blanden had taken up his pilgrim's staff, when the sun was already bending to its decline, and the heat of the day was over; but his own feelings were quite fresh as dawn. Those dreams of first love, which breathed such a wondrous softness over life, had been revived in him once more; he buried himself completely in those reveries.

His thoughts went back to the time when, as a scholar in the upper school, he had been in love with the daughter of a Burgomaster in some country town. He reverted to the emotions which he then felt, as the rattling post-chaise approached the little town at an early morning hour, first rolling over the pavement between the barns of the suburb, then through the empty, sleeping streets, by the lifeless houses, part closed shutters, until he reached the market-place, where stood the house belonging to the town's functionary, which, with its faded pink colouring, blushed more joyously in the morning sunlight.

There, too, an invisible hand pushed the curtain aside, and a little visible, curly head, around one unfinished side of which curl-papers still rustled, looked out, smiling so pleasantly, and nodded its greeting—and the postillion blew a stirring tune, as he stopped before the Black Eagle of the Post-house.

How happy, how blissful was the schoolboy's heart! That moment in which the angel's head nodded to him out of its concealment, caused him greater ecstacies than any happiness of a later extravagant love, and never had the heart's throbs of expectant longing been more vivid than in the post-chaise at that time!

Now it seemed to him as if he were capable of similar emotions, as if, after internal regeneration, the youth's singleness of heart were returning again for a short period.

The longing for his campanula lent wings to his steps, he saw her picture vividly before him; the flying shadows of the clouds did not bear it away with them; the Samland "Palven"[1] which extended on the left side of the road, that dead heath with its solitary bushes, that chilling sterility and barrenness of nature did not subdue his spirits, and the resounding thunder of the surf, sometimes near, sometimes more distant, stirred the wanderer's heart and steps to move at a merry pace.

Evening's crimson light sparkled in the valley's ravines and brooks, which flow on towards the sea; upon the tops of the oaks and beeches, above the steep, jagged cliffs; in the luxuriant vallies; upon the bare heights and above the glimpses of the swelling ocean which the eye discovers either between groups of trees towering up on nigh, or away over the sand-hills.

This melancholy light, which encourages the mind's return to the past, to half-forgotten scenes, did not harmonise with the wanderer's mood; a fresh, sparkling, dewy morning, with a cool breeze from the coast of the enterprise-loving Scandinavians, or the islands of the old Vikings, would have satisfied it better.

Blanden wished to break with his past, even drive away all the thoughts that reminded him of it; his Eva, whom he had found by the woodland stream, should be to him as the first woman of creation, whom he meets, to whom yields his undesecrated feelings.

This love should be to him as a draught from a fresh spring, refreshing, cooling, and at the same time metamorphosing him as if by mysterious magic.

Was it, then, love? It was in the first instance only a brief meeting; but it dropped the seed of love into his heart, and it was his will to nourish and cultivate that seed.

As he walked along, lost in such thoughts, the rays of the evening sun disappeared suddenly beneath heavy clouds, through which at first it peeped like a flaming triumphal arch, until the increasing shades of night enveloped the extinguished glow.

At the same time a storm arose, which burst in the wooded defiles with furious rapidity, so that the cracking of broken boughs under foot denoted his path, while the thunder of the sea became louder and more portentous, and the thousand crests of waves rose higher towards the heavy, lowering clouds.

Soon the thunder of the sky amalgamated with the thunder of the billows; lightning glided down the sharp, rugged hills along the coast, so that their singular profiles gleamed like demons' faces. The lonely "Palven" bushes shivered in the tempest, and the whole heath seemed to be in ghost-like motion.

Blanden felt himself refreshed by this magnificent spectacle of Nature; he thought of the proud grandeur and immutability of the universe.

Just so did the storm sweep over the verdure of the heath, waving to and fro, just so did the sea cast its foaming surf against the cliffs when the ancient

Prussians still lived here, who in the grove of Romove, sacrificed to their god Perkunos; when the knights of orders, their cloaks above their armour, and the black cross upon their white mantles, rode upon their steeds along the coast, when the Holy Virgin and the old heathen deity stood opposed in irreconcilable conflict.

Then the din of battle raged above the Baltic shore, as to-day the din of the unfettered elements; yet, how everything had been changed!

What would the heathens say to the towns abounding with churches, which had driven out their sacred groves; what the knights of the orders to the disciplined regiments whose close columns belch forth fire, while flying batteries hasten to the heights to hurl death forth to a distance formerly undreamed of? Yet one visible, red thread never lost, extends through all changes of time. That which energetic and highly-gifted Masters of Orders had attempted for the cultivation of the land, when they made the wide plains arable, protected the marshes against the onslaught of the tide by means of dykes, appointed a secure bed for the streams, was a heritage to which the Hohenzollern princes succeeded, and made fruitful unto the present day.

The sudden breaking of the tempest even drew Blanden's mind momentarily from the immediate emotions which had possession of it, but as the clouds, too, opened their sluices, and thunder followed closely upon the lightning's footsteps as it leaped dazzlingly across the path, then the open air became intolerable, and the wanderer turned into the first tavern.

It was a fisherman's ale-house, whose exterior promised but little hospitable reception. Yet several carts stood in a half-open shed, and numerous baskets were piled up, denoting that there was no lack here of commercial traffic.

Despite the weather, the little windows in the large parlour stood open, and, in the pauses which the thunder made, a confused noise was emitted of men's quarrelling voices, between them the high pitched tones of a woman, who evidently sought to establish quiet in this uproar.

A rain-drenched trap stood unwatched before the door; the horse, with limply drooping mane, shied at the lightning without causing the heavy waggon to move from its position.

Two parties stood opposite one another in the small tavern parlour; gleaming pieces of amber, of the most beautiful pale-yellow shade, lay upon the table; on the right-hand, in the background of the room, several washtubs could be seen, in which the fishermen, with their brawny, naked arms, sought to cleanse the produce of the pits on the shore from the soil that clung to it.

But one of the men had just now left this occupation. With menacing gesture, with clenched fist, he stood erect, his face glowing with anger, and appeared to be repudiating some accusation that was hurled against him by a man with a remarkable countenance, who leaned upon the table containing the pieces of amber. The two other fishermen certainly continued to wash the primeval resin in their tubs, at the same time, however, taking part in the dispute with violent words.

The stranger who, with folded arms, opposed an iron determination to this fury of the Baltic Masanielli, was very uncommon looking. His dress was slightly Russian. His two companions who stood beside him, were clad entirely in national costume; but his features betokened a southern origin.

He had the fiery eye of an Italian; his whole figure might have led one to take him for one of those *principe*, who, at the feast of *Corpus Christi*, ride on splendid horses behind the Pope, as his *guardia nobile*. Only a wilder expression lay in his features, dark overhanging eye-brows, sharp lines about mouth and nose, told of abundant evil passionate experiences.

"I counted the pieces accurately in the pit," he cried to the shouting fishermen, "I looked closely at them. One was large enough to make a pretty toilet casket, and that piece is missing; it has been suppressed in washing!"

The fishermen's muscular hands were raised again in denial of this accusation. The fisherman's wife, in red headkerchief and green woollen dress, interposed, saying that there should be no disturbance in her parlour; the piece had, perhaps, fallen from the waggon, and would be found after all.

"It is a disgrace to accuse honest people falsely!" cried the ring-leader of the amber-washers, whilst a gleam of yellow lightning flashed, and a quickly-following clap of thunder awoke the echo of the cliffs.

Blanden had listened to the dispute at the open door. Then he entered, and his sudden appearance caused the noise to cease.

"Landlady!" cried he, "a drink to refresh me! And you people, can you not agree quietly? Do not the heavens make commotion enough? Spirits and beer for these good people; for to-day they have carted sand, and washed amber enough—they need refreshment! Hang my coat before the kitchen stove, best of women! The old Samland gods have washed my skin!"

"Who are you, my Herr?" cried the amber merchant, "that you issue orders here, and withhold my washermen from their work?"

"Grant them a short rest," said Blanden, as he seated himself in his shirt sleeves at the table upon which gleamed the pale yellow gifts of the East Sea. "Perhaps we, too, may do some business, my good sir; I am just in the humour to-day to buy the Great Mogul's diamonds."

The Italian became more friendly; still, however, he regarded the interloper with a distrustful glance. His two companions, with their slit Calmuck eyes, permitted themselves to grin pleasantly. They looked meaningly at the fishermen, who were already refreshing themselves with the liquor which the hostess had given them.

Blanden understood how to acknowledge their friendliness, and recommended them also to the landlady's care.

Now a deep silence reigned. Blanden examined the pieces of amber; the dealer looked at him with a keen glance, and once started back as if startled, when Blanden's features were illumined by a sharp flash of lightning. It seemed as if some sudden recollection had dawned within him. The keen glances with which from henceforth he regarded the other, however, bore no tokens of amity about them.

"You come from Russia?" the nobleman began his enquiries, while he weighed a large piece of amber in his hands.

"From Wilna, my Herr."

"But you are no Russian?"

"I am an Italian."

"I took you for one. I love the Italians! They are a gifted people! What a pity that many years of oppression keeps their noble fire in subjection, so that it only finds vent for itself in petty, malicious outbreaks, like the flames of their Solfatara! An Italian—and how do you come to Russia?"

"Business connections. A merchant remains there where he has most prospect of gain."

"Then the amber trade between these coasts and Russia is probably flourishing?"

"It depends," said the stranger, with a cunning smile, "whether a man succeeds in bringing his wares cheaply across the frontier. Besides, the peasants, who have farmed their royalty from Government, are not exactly reasonable with their amber, let them dig it out of the earth with spades, or rescue it from the sea-weed, or obtain it with dragnets from the sea."

"What reflections might it not awake," said Blanden to himself, and hardly noticing the others. "The forests of other days have sunk beneath the earth, and still offer their treasures to the living race—but what becomes of our sunken hopes? They have nothing, nothing more to give us! Ah! if any one could dream so deeply, so utterly deeply, he might hear the rustling of the trees in the submarine forests, and see sitting there the amber nymph in magnificent jewels of the deep, in those pale-yellow halls, and singing a song of the old splendours of the never-penetrated forests, into which the complaints of men have never yet taken refuge."

And, as he looked more closely at the vision of the amber-nymph, it bore Eva's features, and he resolved to deck her worthily of his vision.

"But what shall I do with this rough, raw material?" said he, petulantly, to the dealer, "I cannot buy any of this from you; at the most, only the little piece which contains the imprisoned fly. Oh, happy he, who might sit so firmly in a woman's heart!"

They agreed about the not insignificant price of this rarity; the dealer then began—

"I see clearly that only the artistically formed produce of the ocean has any value for you. Yet I know first-rate masters in Wilna to whom I sell my wares, and who know how to lend every delicate form to them. Give me commissions! When I return I will certainly bring you everything that you can wish to your complete satisfaction."

"And when do you return?"

"In a few weeks."

Blanden considered for a moment, then he said—

"Well, then, you shall procure me an outfit for an amber princess; everything of pale-yellow, most precious material. Take out your pocket-book, and make notes. First, a tasteful toilet casket, fragrant as the Oriental beauties love it; then a splendid string of beads—the beads of our Northern Ocean shall shame the corals of the Southern Sea; a bracelet; a brooch with two winged doves, or a little Cupid with a dart. Can the master's art produce any other such perfections that are fitted for beauty's adornment, even if it does not hover before my own imagination, here am I, a ready purchaser."

"I should, of course, always find a sale for such goods," said the dealer, "yet may I ask your name?"

Blanden told his name and that of his castle. The Italian wrote both down; a triumphant expression lay in the slight smile around the corners of his mouth, in his piercing glances; he himself gave his card, upon which stood the name, Carlo Baluzzi, of Wilna.

Blanden's thoughts meanwhile lingered with his campanula: "A flower-fairy she appeared to me," thought he to himself; "the original child of Nature! For me she shall become an amber-nymph! All my past life shall

44

remain deeply buried beneath the high, rising tide; but its tears shall be made into beads which shall adorn her."

In the meantime the storm without had passed away, but the darkness of the tempest's clouds had been succeeded by the darkness of the evening.

The fishermen returned to their work; the landlady lighted a few dripping tallow candles; Baluzzi's eye rested upon the tubs, that not a piece which he had bought so dearly might be lost to him.

Blanden took leave; notwithstanding the well-meaning coal-stove, his coat was wet through and through, but no choice remained to him.

"Farewell, Herr von Blanden," said the Italian, with sharp emphasis. "I am pleased to have renewed my acquaintance with you."

"Renewed?" asked Blanden, astonished.

"Yes, my Herr."

"And where have you seen me?"

"On Lago Maggiore, two years ago."

"I do not recollect—"

"Nor is it possible! The pleasure was entirely on my side! You lived then in such sunshine of bliss that you did not notice the two shadows in the background, which hastened quickly past you."

Blanden, while he walked shiveringly along through the chilly evening air, meditated vainly what connection there could have been between Baluzzi and himself during his stay by Lago Maggiore.

What did those peculiar looks signify, which he suddenly assumed? What should the remarkable emphasis mean which he gave to his words—yes, the enmity which gleamed in his features—in his whole demeanour?

After mature reflection, Blanden came to the conclusion that he must have been mistaken if he sought to ascribe any special importance to a chance meeting.

But when Blanden had left the room, the Italian rubbed his hands together with scornful satisfaction.

"Now I, too, shall learn," said he to himself, "what has become of her, and my old receipts will flow in once more."

45

CHAPTER VI.

ON LAND AND SEA.

A sparkling, dewy morning made Warnicken, that jewel of the Samland coast, glisten with double brilliancy.

Blanden stood beneath the oaks of the precipitous declivity of the Fuchs-spitze. Impatiently he followed the slowly rising course of the sun and the shadows gradually moving aside.

Slowly the tops of the trees stood out one after another in the sunny light, and the course of the heavenly orb could be measured beneath them in the green verdure, in which the quivering, leafy network spun its shadows ever farther over the campanulas, whose calix had just now glittered in the sunny illumination.

Every branch, every flower, became a hand of the sun's clock for the impatient tarrier, while its seconds and minutes moved haltingly forward.

Blanden's disquiet was not the consequence of that longing with which joyous, triumphant love goes to a reunion. A single meeting may make a deep impression on the heart, but yet it only yields an uncertain picture, more resembling a vision, than tangible reality, and how much still is left to the enquiring mind; how easily is a delusion possible, which lends a lasting value to a transitory mood!

Will the second meeting uphold that which the first one promised? Will it confirm the deep impression which Blanden had received of the campanula in the forest's gloom?

He hardly dared to doubt it; this doubt would have made him unhappy already; because he believed himself to have found that which would be able to give rest and peace to his life.

He hoped for a chance encounter, which might be looked for with certainty in the so little frequented Warnicken; he would not as yet introduce himself into the house, to the family; he dreaded lest its middle-class setting should rob his fancy's picture of its entrancing magic, nor did he feel justified at present in displaying his interest in the girl in so conspicuous a manner.

Morning's freshness, however, did not seem to be beloved by the Warnicken visitors. For a long time no living beings showed themselves.

46

At last Blanden saw the shimmer of a summer dress through the bushes; his heart beat, as if it must be Eva; but it was an old maid in a washed-out morning toilet, carrying a yapping lap-dog, casting a few indifferent glances at the sea, and retiring immediately again, after this modest enjoyment of nature.

Below, by the rope, a bald-headed male visitor splashed in the but slightly-disturbed waves; everything else was quiet and tranquil.

Blanden walked uneasily up and down. Perhaps the whole colony had made some excursion; he would return to the inn to make enquiries about Regierungsrath Kalzow, as chance, upon which he had at first calculated, did not favour him.

The sea, after yesterday's storm, lay in sunny clearness and calm; the splashing of the breakers on the strand only rose like a gentle murmur; merely a slight quiver spread over the vast surface; one hardly knew whether it was the shadow of a cloud flying past, or the pulse's gentle throb of the slumbering sea itself.

Then Blanden perceived a boat being put off from the shore; two girls sat in it, one of whom rowed, while the other, in a clear voice, sang a merry song.

He took his telescope to his aid; a fisher-girl was rowing, but the other was gazing out steadily over the sea. He could not see her features, but he did see that a wreath of blue-bells adorned her straw hat. There, she turned round and directed her face towards the cliffs along the coast; the morning sun lay full upon those fresh features—it was his campanula!

Quickly resolved, Blanden hastened down the steep footpath from the Fuchs-spitze to a landing-place, where two boats still lay at anchor.

He had soon made his bargain with the fisherman: to the latter's great astonishment, he had bought the one for a price which richly compensated him for the temporary loss.

Quickly as lightning, Blanden sprang into the boat, seized the oar, and followed the skiff, which was already disappearing in the distance. The vigorous physical exertion made him feel his internal impatience less keenly.

"I seem to myself," thought he, "to be like an old pirate-prince, who gives chase to a beautiful woman. The confounded stillness of the sea! If I could only set full sail, so as to hasten more speedily after my sweet prey. But no quarter when once I have boarded the enemy's ship!"

Blanden pulled with all his might, and the distance between him and the two girls' skiff did indeed become ever smaller; it appeared, too, as though they were about to turn round, they watched the boat following them, and sought to avoid it; all the more determinedly did it pursue their evading movements.

The one girl stood erectly in the skiff, her hand resting on the rudder; she looked in curious expectance at the persistent pursuer, while the other girl rowed on with stolid indifference.

Blanden, with the art of a skilled sailor, cut off every possible means of return; so that farther flight seaward only remained. Both girls seemed to be agreed on that point; Eva's signs and actions left no doubt about it; but it was already too late: by attempting to return they had lost too much of their start, and Blanden, in his little boat, pulled, with great strength and rapidity.

"Campanula!" cried he to her, when they had come near enough to one another; she recognised his voice. As in sweet alarm, she let the tiller ropes slip from her hands; then she stood motionlessly and folded them. But the fisher-girl commenced a spasmodic race, in vain Eva signed and called to her; the girl only nodded her head and pulled on, but Blanden after a short time overtook them once more.

"Captured at last!" cried he triumphantly, "difficult as it is made for us to greet an old acquaintance again!"

"Welcome, Herr Assistant!" cried Eva, who had recovered her unaffected liveliness, "I admire your knowledge of seamanship; you probably have gained it in duck-shooting?"

"Do you not find, my beautiful child," said Blanden, "that this conversation is somewhat uncomfortable, and at the same time, dangerous? Our boats are so close together, that they might knock against and upset one another, and I shall not stir from your side any more, after having worked my way into your vicinity by the sweat of my brow."

"What is to be done then?" asked Eva, "we shall go down together."

"Oh, no, I shall act according to the rights of the sea!"

"Have you some kind of right on your side again? Are you an inspector of the sea perhaps, as you were inspector of the forest, and would you ask me again for my passport?"

"The right which I have on my side, is one of the oldest and best rights which history knows; it is the right of might! I shall take possession of your boat and declare it, with all that it contains, to be a lawful prize. You are sailing without a flag, you have no ship's papers."

"And do we live in time of war?"

"Certainly until we have made peace, I see a lovely enemy in you; therefore—board and give no quarter!"

And with a rapid bound Blanden had sprung into Eva's violently rocking boat, while he relinquished his own to the waves.

The weak minded fisher-girl, with a low cry, pointed to the boat floating away, while she exclaimed—

"Father's boat! Father's boat!"

"Indeed," said Eva, as she retired completely to the rudder, "you are not wanting in audacity? This is an attack in pirate fashion!"

"Do I look like a corsair?"

"I do not know any personally, but why should you not sit for the frontispiece to Byron's poem? You are sun-burnt enough for it, and look as though you would have no fear of adventures!"

"Certainly not, if the prize be worth the risk!"

"And then—how recklessly you treat the property of others! The poor fisherman's boat drifts upon the waves, without a master."

"Excuse me, my Fräulein! That boat is my property; I bought it and can give it up again to the billows."

"And why do you do this?"

"Is it not worth some sacrifice to be with you? Nor would I appear here as lord and master; no, but as your humble oarsman! Away little one, let me go to the oar."

The fisher-girl did not stir; seeing he was about to take the oar from her by force, she prepared to stand upon the defensive.

"Let the poor child alone," said Eva, "she will not leave her post."

Blanden hesitated; suddenly the girl voluntarily relinquished the oar, cried again twice in a shrieking voice—

"Father's boat! Father's boat!" and then plunged into the sea. Blanden was about to jump after her.

"Do not," said Eva, "she is the best swimmer in all the villages on the coast; but she is imbecile, and only seldom has gleams of reason."

"And you trust yourself to her?" asked Blanden.

"No one pulls so good an oar, has better knowledge of wind and weather and of the sea's peculiarities; she is a water spirit with her meaningless frog's eyes. I should rely most implicitly upon her in every danger of the stormy sea. Only look how she swims; she has reached the forsaken boat, swings herself into it, and grasps the oar!"

"That is disagreeable enough for me!" said Blanden.

"Why in the world?"

"If you would take my telescope, lovely child, you would perceive that a large number of glasses are directed towards us from the Fuchs-spitze, although a short time ago, the most solemn silence reigned beneath the Perkunos oaks. People are observing us, and will observe us still more—what will they say, if Fräulein Eva sails upon the sea with a stranger."

"You are right," said Eva, suddenly blushing deeply, "but what has that to do with your boat?"

"Very much, my Fräulein! If the latter floated quietly away on the sea, we might relate a credible tale of how it had leaked and I had taken refuge in your safer boat; that stupid child has deprived us of this fiction because she will row the skiff, uninjured back to the shore."

"Then you must invent another tale," said Eva.

"Why should I not sing and tell of a Baltic Lorelei, at sight of whom the boatman in the little boat is seized with wild melancholy, to whom he is irresistibly drawn."

"Because that boatman with his little boat is not swallowed up."

"Heine only fears it, my Fräulein; it need not therefore happen, and as yet we do not know the end of this little story. But just look; a whole girls' school seems to have assembled on the Fuchs-spitze and below also on the landing place I see visitors."

"I fear, they are my father and mother," said Eva, "they have already always forbidden these sailing expeditions; but I cannot give them up. Such a morning's row upon the sea refreshes me so wonderfully; one seems to glide onwards into eternity upon these deep, quiet waves; above the wide heavens, beneath the increasing abyss, the farther we retire from the safe shore; and where the billows meet the sky, even there the world does not end; it only seems to do so! Far away beyond, extends the longing for other shores, for other people! There the sailing ships, the steam boats, distant, stately pass by from harbour to harbour. How large the world is! And thus surrounded with the splashing of chattering waves, with the fresh breeze wafted from afar, there I have quite different, better thoughts, than yonder amidst mankind, that is always gossiping of trivial, everyday matters, criticising dress, depriving itself of the small respect due to it."

"Bravo, my Lorelei!" cried Blanden, "the sailor shares these thoughts and feelings with his mermaid, he rejoices that he really bears a mermaid in his boat, not one of those ordinary land young ladies, who even in the face of eternity, only think of their own little wares, of their possessions and belongings, dresses and bonnets, ribbons and bows, and who believe that their passenger ticket upon earth has merely been given to them on account of their goods. But father and mother—there some slight justification is due. Did you tell them of our late meeting?"

"No," said Eva, blushing.

"And why not?"

Eva was silent.

"Our adventure in the wood was too unimportant, or you forgot it quickly?"

"Oh, no," said Eva; "but visits without visiting cards are not announced."

"Good; then we have one little secret between us, and our sea excursion is another. I shall explain that I believed you to be in danger, as a half-witted girl rowed your boat, and that I therefore changed places."

During this conversation they had neared the shore. The Regierungsrath was running angrily up and down, his hands in his coat-pockets; the large, white cravat in which he had buried his chin seemed to be loosely twined round it to-day, and moved to and fro.

His massive wife was more self-possessed, but an ominous lecture lay in her eyes, and about the corners of her mouth.

"Oh, Eva," she cried to her daughter, as soon as her voice could be at all audible without the aid of a speaking trumpet.

Blanden pulled to the shore, sprang out, bound the boat firmly to a post, offered his hand to assist Eva to descend, and then busied himself with the boat and oars, while Eva had to let the first hurricane of reproaches and reproof sweep over her.

"And, who, then, is this strange gentleman?" asked old Kalzow, with the air of an inquisitor.

Eva shrugged her shoulders.

"It is too bad, though," stormed her mother; "a *tête-à-tête* upon the sea with a perfect stranger!"

"He only introduced himself to me as a pirate, who had boarded my ship."

"No, my Fräulein," said Blanden, now stepping nearer; "I believed you to be in danger. One ought not to venture upon the sea with an idiot girl."

"There you are right," said the Regierungsrath, suddenly appeased by the stranger coinciding with him, and also reproaching his imprudent daughter.

The former's fashionable appearance made a favourable impression upon the old gentleman, who, as an introduction to friendly relations, offered him a pinch of snuff.

Blanden thanked him with a slight bow.

"Our meeting upon the ocean waves, my Fräulein, was of so poetical a character that I feared to desecrate it by the prose of social forms; permit me, therefore, now only to introduce myself to you and your family. My name is Blanden—Max von Blanden."

The Regierungsrath gave his name.

"I have an additional pleasure in making your acquaintance if you are a relation of that old gentleman to whom the magnificent estates, Rossitten, Kulmitten, and Nehren belong. I used often to be in that neighbourhood; I know the estates, because they border upon a district whither my official duties sometimes lead me; I am, namely, in the third division of the Government, Woods and Forests—that is my branch! Thus I have seen the old proprietor once or twice, and heard his beautiful estates much talked about—a pleasant gentleman."

"All praise that he receives, honours and gratifies me, because I am his son!"

"His son!" said the Regierungsrath, with a friendly chuckle; "then you probably manage that extensive property."

"Certainly, and entirely upon my own account; because my poor, good-hearted father now contents himself with a very small portion of it."

"Then he has resigned most of the estates to you?" said the Regierungsräthin, who looked upon the promising heir with especial good will.

"All, all, *gnädige* Frau! He only claims one very small place—the place in the Blandens' family vault—he died half a year ago!"

"Oh, how sad!" said the *gnädige* Frau, with a sigh, while, speedily consoled, she added—

"Then in you we recognise the heir and owner of these beautiful possessions."

"Alas! I cannot alter it, little talent as I have hitherto displayed in exercising my rights of ownership in a becomingly solemn manner."

The result of this examination was a brilliant one. Rath and Räthin were seized with internal disquiet as to how they could best ensure themselves this gratifying acquaintance for some time. They looked at one another with questioning and answering glances.

Eva was too happy; she did not know why. She concerned herself but little about the master and owner of the property; but the friendly footing between her parents and Blanden made her very happy.

For a moment she might be vexed with him that he had enveloped himself in mystery towards her, and had not even told her his name; this fleeting sensation of anger soon passed tracelessly away.

The world lay so seemingly bright before her; she could have sung, shouted, danced, had it not been so very contrary to propriety; but she could not quite restrain her exuberant spirits.

Half-witted Käthe landed just at that moment with her father's boat; dripping with wet, she sprang upon the shore.

Eva liked the poor girl, in whom there was something heroic, resolute; it was painful to her that the brave child believed herself to have rescued something, while by her plunge into the sea and her skill in rowing, she had only brought a stranger's boat into the haven; and when the little one, with radiant eyes, stepped towards Eva, and with a triumphant smile, pointed to the skiff which she had rowed to the shore, the former embraced the girl—she was so full of her own happiness that others' misfortunes touched her doubly. Certainly, she had not considered the consequences, as the embrace had rendered her morning toilet so wet that she shivered with the cold damp, and her mother scoldingly bade her go home to change her clothes.

First, however, Herr von Blanden was invited to share the modest mid-day meal at the inn, as well as accompany them to the forest, on an afternoon excursion, which had been arranged with other visitors. His acceptance made her parents and Eva equally happy.

On their road home, the Regierungsrath calculated to his wife what the average revenue of the Rositten, Kulmitten and Nehren estates would be, trying to draw the correct medium of income between favourable and unfavourable years. He knew the nature of the soil, the number of acres; the result worked out in ponderous figures was received by the Frau Räthin with a well-pleased smile.

Eva had hastened on in front; yet her parents' conversation was confined to income, taxes, and other questions of national economy. No discussion was needed, for they understood one another.

Suddenly Frau Räthin stayed her winged steps; daring hopes and plans had lent a more lively movement to her usually majestic gait; but a rising thought suddenly paralysed it in a most disturbing manner.

"Gracious heavens!" cried she, as she supported herself with her parasol against an old oak trunk.

"What is the matter with you, Miranda?" asked her husband anxiously.

"We have invited him—and have quite forgotten the one thing!"

"The poor dinner, do you mean? Oh, people are used to that at the seaside; Spartan fare is the rule here!"

"No, no! We have forgotten to ask—"

"What then, in the world?"

"If Herr von Blanden is not already married?"

The Regierungsrath's chin jumped into his cravat with a slight shock of alarm.

"You are right, Miranda! We are very foolish!"

"He is no longer a youth; I should put him down as being thirty years old, and a man of that age, of his brilliant position, looked up to, rich—nothing else can be possible—he must have had a wife long since!"

Lost in sad thought, both walked silently side by side.

"But if I consider it properly," said Kalzow, "it cannot well be so. He would have taken his wife with him to the sea."

"People do not always take their wives with them to bathing-places."

"And then, he showed such evident interest in Eva! It has not been exactly explained yet how that occurrence took place at sea. Did you hear what Eva said about the buccaneer? He boarded, captured her, I don't know what else! Let us hope that it was all right."

"We should hope so? You talk of boarding and capturing—and on that account Herr von Blanden must be unmarried? Old man—we know better! Many an one has laid siege and taken captive who should not have gone out to steal, because he has a good wife at home. And you, too, old man, if one knew everything! But you should not pretend such innocence, when your daughter's happiness is concerned!"

This turn to the conversation was plainly disagreeable to the Regierungsrath; he took several pinches of snuff quickly one after another, and sought to bring about an understanding with his wife, by devising a plan of campaign, how to-day at dinner, even before the pudding arrived, they might tear aside the veil which shrouded Herr von Blanden's domestic circumstances.

They were agreed on one point, that if he were guilty of the crime of being married already, he should be treated accordingly, and all further intercourse be coolly broken off.

In the meanwhile, the hero of this discussion still stood on the shore, and studied the wet ocean curiosity with its goggle eyes, which he could picture perfectly to himself as one of those subordinate fish-goddesses who flounder about Neptune's car. He tried in vain to make her understand about his boat. The old fisherman came forward and rated the girl for the boldness with which she had taken possession of another person's property.

Blanden made her a present of the boat, and gradually, with silent delight, she comprehended that she had become its owner. Then he pressed a piece of gold into her hand, and its flashing shimmer transported idiot Käthe into a perfect tumult of happiness. She held it in the sun, and at the same time danced in a circle round it, until the fisherman reminded her of the duty of returning thanks for it.

She hastened to Blanden, kissed his hands, and looked at him with eyes whose glassy glitter was brightened with a moist gleam.

The second meeting with Eva had only strengthened Blanden in his hopes and wishes. She appeared to be as sensible and beautiful as the first time; as fresh, pure, and frank as he had imagined the wife of his choice. At the same time, she was not without mental ability; not so slow and apathetic as such calm and beautiful natures often are. She was not consumed by commonplace, insignificant ideas, in which, from the character of their bringing up, the daily associations, the depressing example, talents of a higher organisation are often stifled.

Father and mother had made careful arrangements for the dinner in the modest inn; the daughter, however, remained in reserve until the ground had been properly reconnoitred.

Blanden was appointed to a seat by the mother, while the daughter sat on the other side of her father. These precautionary measures astonished him slightly; he did not imagine that he must first prove himself to be a man towards whom it was possible to entertain serious intentions.

The conversation turned upon politics, which, at that time, were the salt of every East Prussian dinner-table. The Regierungsrath pushed his vedettes carefully forward, and, with the vanguard of his articles of belief, made a retrograde movement, as he remarked that a superior enemy's force stood before him.

Not on any account would he injure his cause with Herr Von Blanden, and manifested himself a temperate, tolerant man, to the great amazement of the Kreisgerichtsrath sitting opposite to him, with whom he had often broken a lance at table over these very questions.

"We are not yet ripe for a constitution," said Kalzow, "at least, not for a constitution according to the modern English and French form. We are a patriarchal people, and what would become of our bureaucracy if Parliament should speak the decisive words? In England and France it is quite different; there they have no such official power representing the intelligence of the whole State, yes, which, as it were, it has absorbed within itself. I cannot imagine a Prussia with a constitutional organisation: we shall never live to see that, little as I fail to recognise the advantages of such institutions."

"But, my dear friend," interposed the Kreisgerichtsrath, "you have always hurled unqualified anathemas at them."

"It depends upon the nature of the soil, dear friend," replied the Regierungsrath; "elsewhere these plants may thrive capitally, it is impossible with us."

"I cannot see that," said Blanden, "I believe that we, too, shall one day occupy the position that is due to us amongst Europe's nations, if we become the equals of advanced peoples by means of a free constitution. Until then, I hesitate to count Prussia amongst the leading civilised states. The bureaucracy alone, best of Regierungsraths, cannot assist us to it. I have travelled far over the world, I know the Celestial Empire."

"You mean China?" interrupted the Räthin. Unbroken silence reigned around.

"Yes, *gnädige* Frau, and I assure you that officialdom is excellently organised there. The candidate undergoes his examination before the *Wald der Pinsel*,[2] in Nankin."

"*Wald der Pinsel?*" asked the Regierungsrath.

"So is the college for examinations designated there."

"That term of ridicule has surely been invented by some candidate who failed," suggested the Gerichtsrath.

"It is no term of ridicule," explained Blanden, "it is the official designation. The Chinese, it is well known, write with brushes, and this *Wald der Pinsel* is as well versed in all the old books of law and history, in the philosophical writings of Con-fut-se and La-ot-se, as any European University's Senate is at home in the works of all the professions. I will not assert that these men are specially intelligent—that is to say, I mean the Chinese *Wald der Pinsel*, not the European—but they are learned, pedantic, and so strict in examination, that many a bachelor who has, perhaps, paid more homage to a lover with a green girdle than to the muses, fails irretrievably."

"I was not aware," said the Regierungsrath, "that they possessed institutions in China betokening such high cultivation."

"Oh, they have a great many of them," continued Blanden, "the different grades of Mandarins have buttons on their caps. It is thus known at once if one of these dignitaries is a Chinese assessor, counsellor, chief-counsellor, privy counsellor; and, without asking for his visiting-card, each can immediately be treated with due respect. With us, people sometimes make mistakes about rank; one gives offence, and yet rank is not less esteemed by us than it is in China."

"With reason," said the Regierungsrath; "that which one has earned and merited, one likes to see recognised by the world."

"You see, in the Celestial Empire, everything is arranged in the most excellent manner. Yet this State is a pig-tail State, a marionette State, because the people only count by souls and heads, because all intellectual life and action, every right, every liberty, is wanting. The Celestial son rules it by the rod of his officials. Everything blooms and flourishes, but it is a lacquered happiness, all paper and tinsel rubbish, a crushing existence of formula. What I saw there of the law and Government reminds me of the Kasperle Theatre; they chop off heads with the same equanimity as that with which Kasperle disposes of his enemies—human life has no value, dignity of man is unknown."

"But that is different with us," said the Regierungsrath, as he assumed a self-conscious bearing, and laid knife and fork aside. "What have we in Prussia, according to your views, in common with the Celestial Empire?"

"The Bureaucracy and patriarchal Government."

"Did I not always say so?" cried the Kreisgerichtsrath, triumphantly, "that is quite my view! I am delighted to receive so worthy an ally."

And, at the same time, he cast a malicious glance at the Regierungsrath, as if at a beaten opponent, so that a flush of anger suffused the latter's face, and he contracted his bushy eyebrows.

"Education," continued Blanden, "is so propagated amongst all classes of the Prussian people, that the introduction of a constitution is indeed no reckless venture; besides, it is the fulfilment of old promises, and will unite the bond between prince and people still more firmly. I shall employ all my powers in this province, with the assistance of my worthy colleagues, so that the military Government of Prussia shall become a constitutional one. It will not lose its warlike energy by these means. I say, openly, that this is my dearest task in life. I consider our present political condition to be at the same time intolerable and unworthy."

The Regierungsrath crumpled his dinner-napkin convulsively in his hand; the challenge was too daring. He would gladly have given annihilating expression to his opposite conviction; but he reserved it all on the chance that when at the estates of Kulmitten, Rositten and Nehren, he should not need in future to evince any such tender consideration. Meanwhile, he had one of those coughing and choking attacks which sometimes befell him in moments of great agitation, which he was obliged to suppress. Miranda came readily to his assistance, and thought, as the head waitress had already brought the pudding, she must not hesitate any longer to clear up the state of affairs.

"Since when, Herr von Blanden," asked she, with a most unconcerned countenance, "have you returned from your travels?"

"Only half a-year ago."

That sounded consolatory enough, and the Regierungsrath's condition visibly improved.

"Then, probably," continued the Regierungsräthin, as she calmly poured a spoonful of fruit-sauce upon the pudding, "you have already set up a quiet domestic hearth?"

Now it was for Eva, who had listened silently but attentively, and sympathising warmly with Blanden's remarks to the former conversation, to become pale. She started at the thought that she had never put this question to herself; it lay in a measure so near, and yet so far, from her heart. In breathless tension, she waited for the reply; her heart beat eagerly, yet the firm conviction dwelled within her that Blanden could not yet be fettered.

"The domestic hearth of a bachelor," replied Blanden.

These few words exercised a cheering effect upon the Kalzow family. The Regierungsrath had already mobilised a line of victorious arguments against Blanden's reprehensible political views; they were ready to advance at the double so soon as the signal was given. The attack should commence at dessert, if the declaration of war need not be withheld on account of considerations of policy. This was now the case; everything was disembodied; the most telling proofs were dismissed to their homes; the peaceful mood prevailed so completely, that the Regierungsrath condescended to the most extensive admissions as regards politically emancipated nations. The Kreisgerichtsrath, however, stared anew at the Caudine Passes into which his opponent's logic seemed to have wandered. The Regierungsräthin was seized with a most unusual love of enterprise; she made the most various plans and projects, and first thought over an arrangement of the afternoon party, which should give the young people in the forest the utmost liberty possible for an undisturbed meeting. Eva herself was happy; her life was sunnily bright again. The lowering shadow had passed away without dimming it.

The walk in the forest was undertaken in the happiest mood; the little party of seaside visitors had furnished itself with everything that was necessary. Knitting; packets of coffee and sugar, cakes of every kind, formed the provisions which the careful mothers carried with them, concerning themselves less about the sacred shadows and dwellings of sweet enchantment, than about the arrangements for the afternoon—coffee, which should be prepared at the hospitable hearth of the little forest house. The tall trees rustled, the birds sang, the flowers bloomed, but the respected ladies only heard the coffee-cups rattle in imagination.

Blanden conversed a great deal with the Rath and Räthin, although he came more and more to the conclusion that the interest which he felt in Eva could not be extended to her parents without an effort. The Rath was a pedant who at heart had only a mind for figures and all worldly matters that could be reduced to calculations; the Räthin, too, was accustomed to look upon everything from its business side. In addition, neither was free from that envy which is often an hereditary evil in officials' families, from the envy of those fortunate persons' incomes which are not restricted to small official salaries: a few sallies upon the rich banker's wife, if she walked on in front at a sufficient distance, upon the ostentatious display of her wealth, upon the attempts at being literary which pervaded the whole house, convinced Blanden that the Kalzow family, despite the consciousness of their exalted position, yet in truth belonged to those unhappy persons who are excluded from all the higher enjoyments of life.

Frau Kalzow had another especial cause for animosity towards her wealthy friend; the latter's son, a boy in the first form at the Kneiphof College, devoted particular attention to Eva, and during the walk would not stir from her side, so that it was rendered almost impossible for Herr von Blanden to approach her, as he wished to do. Frau Kalzow employed every legitimate stratagem to entice the promising Salomon away from Eva; she begged him to gather her a blue flower which she had espied far away in the wood, she lost a needle out of her knitting, and Salomon had to go far, far back along the footpath to find this *corpus delicti*, and restore Frau Räthin's work materials to their entirety; yet he executed all these commissions with great rapidity, and came running back breathlessly, so as to be able to renew his conversation with charming Eva.

"It is remarkable," said he to Eva, "that lyrical poets always praise the woods; I have instituted an album for poetry on the subject, and have been obliged already to buy a third volume from the bookbinder. I can discover nothing particular in a wood; fundamentally it is always the same. Some trunks are darker, others lighter; the leaves larger or smaller, dented or downy, and if one looks through between the stems it always bears the same aspect, and a forester, moreover, certainly only thinks of building or firewood. How different such a wealthy poet's soul! Unfortunately, I do not possess it, my Fräulein; therefore, I make extracts of as much poetry as is possible, so as always to be *au fait* when sensations amidst the forest's verdure are under discussion. Even Schiller, I believe, had no mind for woodland lyrics; how beautifully he might have described Fridolin's walk to the Eisenhammer. Yet not the forest only, the church he depicts to us. He had only feeling for the Bohemian forests, and when he peopled them with living beings, it was not elves and fairies, but robbers! Ah, the robbers, my Fräulein! I understand that thoroughly! And that Amalie! She is my ideal! How she rushes at Franz with her sword—she must have been blonde, on account of the song that she sings to the guitar; no brunette could possess so much enthusiasm."

Thus, with inexhaustible eloquence, Salomon entertained his companion, who was too good-natured to display her impatience, or to stop him with derision. After all he intended to show her attention and kindliness, and how could she have repaid it with ingratitude? Eva possessed the most delicate good feeling; her mother did not understand this, and now was indignant at the patience, or rather confidential manner, with which Eva treated the young scholar. At last she had recourse to a fiendish measure; the Frau Kanzleiräthin's fat daughter, otherwise a nice girl, had always been disposed to make advances to that talkative Salomon, and Frau Kalzow spurred her on to them with great zeal and inciting insinuations.

Minna actually did soon appear on Salomon's other side, while showing him a butterfly that she had caught with her summer hat. The butterfly roused the lad's interest, which he did not, however, extend to Minna herself; on the contrary, all the remarks that he made about the capture were directed to Eva, it only offered him an opportunity to show himself in a more brilliant light to the latter, because he knew the day and night butterflies as accurately as the forest lyrists, and, as the son of wealthy parents, possessed a splendid collection of those insects.

"This is a rare specimen, a *trauer mantel* with violet borders; the *trauer mantel* are distinguished by their borders—Nature has ordained this very wisely; a similar thing occurs with students' caps; the corps which I join is merely distinguished by different borders on its caps from the antagonistic corps with which it always fights. We, too, have our drinking parties my Fräulein, and I preside at these gatherings, but no one as yet has drunk me under the table. But as regards the wisdom of Nature, I find it also imprinted on the Apollo. That butterfly is only found in some few valleys in Silesian and other mountains, which thus possess an especial attraction, and are considered to be worth seeing, and so bring profit to the innkeepers and the inhabitants, for there are more butterfly-seekers than any one would believe, and I know one who even bears caterpillars upon his epaulettes."

Minna was much dejected at the small success of her strategy; deeply shamed, she walked along beside Salomon, casting her good-tempered eyes to the ground, and crushing the poor *trauer mantel's* head to death.

In the meantime the forester's lodge was reached, and while the other ladies prepared the coffee, Frau Kalzow deemed it expedient to invite Herr von Blanden to a little walk to the weeping willow hill, but recollected that she had forgotten the way thither, and requested Eva to accompany them as guide. Frau Kalzow remained modestly in the rear during this walk; Eva and Blanden could exchange thoughts and feelings uninterruptedly, gather flowers, climb little hills to obtain views; Frau Kalzow maintained her communications with the vanguard by occasionally calling to it.

Eva chatted innocently and fondly of her girlish and childish years, of her school days; Blanden thus had a glimpse of a mind clear as crystal, but which was also possessed of a sense and sympathy for everything loftier, for art and nature, and even for the questions of the day; only about one thing she was silent in her confessions, she did not mention that she was merely the Kalzow's adopted child; she did not mention her mother. She had often enough experienced what interruption to friendly relations had been called forth by such allusions, how it was her mother, who without knowing or wishing it, had exercised so cruel an influence upon her young life; she thought with silent emotion of the beautiful melancholy figure, whose picture still hovered before her mind; but the inexplicable estrangement permitted no warmer sensation to rise; as all the world was shy of and avoided remembering her mother, so she, too, only thought of her in quiet dreams, and dreaded calling up any lurking ill if she mentioned that name before others: this unsolved mystery oppressed her soul, this *noli me tangere* of her young life; yet there lay so much brightness in her nature that this one single darkening shadow remained unnoticed.

Blanden felt refreshed and younger by his intercourse with the graceful girl; although so many storms had passed over his internal life, yet one spot remained in it, where the longing for peace, the readiness to welcome a quiet state of happiness, defied all desolation, and starting from that spot, his whole life should take a new form; he felt with intense satisfaction that he was still capable of such happiness as the simplicity of a pure, euphonious nature grants, and therein lay the girl's charm, in the perfect harmony of her character. As her slender figure stood before him, not excessively tall, but yet stately and commanding, girlish but not so thin as girls in boarding schools often are in consequence of too much mental cultivation; as the light of her large eyes beamed above beautiful regular features, so in her were mind and heart also in harmonious unison; the movements of her feelings and thoughts possessed the same grace as her physical actions; it was the invisible spirit of tact and moderation that governed her whole body and mind. Wherever she reigned there this spirit must impress itself upon all who approached her, who stepped within her spell! What a guarantee for happiness, for peace, lay in such dominant grace, in such exquisite euphony! All discordant elements must remain aloof; the recollections of the past could have no power before the magical might of such a presence.

That was the thread which Blanden twined mentally around the nosegay of woodland flowers which Eva presented to him! He had firm faith in his own felicity, if he should ensure it by speedy, decisive choice.

But will the young girl be able to love the much older man? Was her ready trust a proof of love, or not, rather qualified to awaken doubt of it? Because perhaps the delicate reserve of love would have been more reticent towards a companion of her own age; the trust reposed so freely in him was in the experienced, older man who should respect it with friendly counsel. And yet the enthusiastic illumination of the gazelle-like eye often excited sympathy, a slight quiver in her voice and her whole being, whenever he approached her, on pressing her hand in his, which Blanden once ventured to offer her, when she was speaking so sweetly and fervently of her childhood's dreams.

And yet, if Eva did really love him, would it be for her own good? Is the chasm not much too great between the unconscious girl, whose life is spent in one single emotion, and the man who has fought his way through every passion, has weathered life's storms in every latitude, to whom graceless womanhood had often offered sweet temptation, who had also felt the charm of danger that lies in forbidden paths, and who on outlawed ways and in a daring manner had sought to unriddle the dark secret in combining the spirituality with the sensuality of human nature? Was it not cold egotism which strove to purchase its own peace, too dearly perhaps, with the price of that of another human being? Could not, sooner or later, the confessions which he had no right, which it was least of all a duty to make to such innocence, be completed by some chance, by gossiping report; and must not some internal rift gradually extend through the beloved one's heart; must she not suddenly feel that she had built the bridge of her happiness across an unknown abyss, from out of whose depth unnatural spirits arose and spread a gloom over her life?

The more serious the affection which Blanden felt for Eva, the more powerful did these considerations become; yes he walked back by her side with a moody brow.

"You are not cheerful," said Eva, "oh you must not cling to gloomy thoughts! What would I not give if I could banish all sadness out of your life!"

"You are good, my child," said Blanden, as he again pressed her hand, "but oh I am not! True goodness of heart, innocence alone can possess; we others have only momentary touches of it; our good works are often but a species of atonement! If you knew what we have lived through, must live through, who have been so tossed about by fate! Often we ask ourselves, if it is really we who have done this or been guilty of that, it seems so strange, so incredible to us; we would gladly sever the thread which binds the present with the past, but always this self, this indestructible I, that cannot set itself free from its deeds, that often grins at us like a spectre. Even the tree can shake off its withered leaves; but the withered leaves of our life cling indissolubly to us, and no coming spring sweeps them away with its rejuvenating breath."

"You certainly have done no evil," said Eva, "I will be surety for that."

"That surety is bold, my Fräulein; yet, certainly, no evil that is the fruit of internal wickedness, that would intentionally injure the well-being of mankind, nothing from base motives. But from personal error, much evil often arises, and one may ruin those whom one loves!"

"Mutual love knows no ruin," replied Eva, and joyful pride, nameless confidence was expressed in these words, and in her demeanour.

"That is a beautiful belief, and it would be cruel to disturb it."

"Oh, you are kind and good," continued Eva, "despite your strange utterances, which might alarm one; yes, sometimes you have such a scoffing expression, and such an evil gleam in your kindly eyes, that I could be afraid of you myself! Yet, it soon passes away. Has mankind injured you so deeply that you should cherish such hostile emotions?"

"They me, and I them! Thus it is in the world! But I will not soil your pure mind with such thoughts."

Eva and Blanden returned thoughtfully to the forester's lodge, and it was welcome to them that Frau Kalzow, who had joined them again, should now bear the burden of the conversation, as she made several unmistakable allusions to the growing intimacy between Blanden and Eva, and then had recourse to a description of the coffee-party, which did not fail in the sharpest, most characteristic colouring.

The hour for coffee had, however, been missed by the expedition to the weeping willows, and the defaulters had to content themselves with a second infusion of the Mocha beverage.

The next day all the members of the forest party were the guests of Herr von Blanden, who had sent for the best and most expensive wines from Neukuhren.

Consequently, all were in the liveliest spirits; the political debates were carried on as eagerly as could be desired; Blanden even no longer felt melancholy, as he had done on the previous day; he was in a most cheerful humour, and brilliant fireworks of thought entertained the guests, of whom most, however, were but little able to appreciate them.

Eva did not criticise the rapid changes of mood which Blanden displayed. She rejoiced at his gaiety, his exuberant spirits.

In the afternoon an excursion was made to the charming Georgswalder ravine, and there pitched a nomad camp beneath tall oaks and beeches.

Blanden's hesitation of the previous day had disappeared; he only perceived in Eva an eligible, beautiful woman. Boldly he sought and paid her attention, which was not repulsed with any false shame or affected modesty.

On the third day they went again into the forest. Blanden's courtship of Eva had not been unobserved, as was betokened plainly enough by the prevailing disposition of the guests.

While the Regierungsrath and his friends rejoiced over it, a hostile, rancorous party was not wanting.

The Kanzleiräthin deemed Eva's behaviour extremely unbecoming and would have given Herr von Blanden credit for better taste, or, at least, more discrimination, as a man of his years ought not to pay attention to so young a girl: her dear Minna was six or eight years older; the habit of making false statements about the year of her birth and baptismal certificate, had made her mother herself uncertain about it.

Minna possessed that steadiness which is befitting a good housewife; her physical beauty also was perfectly capable of bearing comparison with that of slender Eva, as her figure was plump, and her eyes were not full of that unhealthy enthusiasm which Eva's too large pupils betrayed.

And then, Minna owned a mother who rejoiced in an immaculate character; Eva, certainly, had two such relations, but the present one, a mother according to the country's laws, is disagreeable enough, and about the other it is best to be silent.

Minna herself was too good-hearted to feel envy or jealousy; she was only mournful, and Salomon once found her in tears, sitting beneath the weeping willows.

He did not so calmly bear the unworthy preference which Eva granted to an elderly gentleman, who surely already belonged to the Philistines, instead of bestowing her favours upon fresh, joyous youth.

It is true, Eva had never been unfriendly towards him, but what was this friendliness to him?

Young wealthy Salomon might count upon occupying the first place in the heart of a Regierungsrath's daughter. Herr von Blanden might also be rich, but was he as young and had he such a future before him as Salomon?

"It is incredible, mamma!" said he to his sympathising mother, "they are walking together again, talking confidentially. That Blanden, who is more than thirty years old, and has passed through many a storm, and what has he done in the world? Certainly, he has a cut upon his right cheek, a proof that he has studied; but apart from that cut he has gained hardly any merit, and can he actually be termed handsome, mamma?"

"He is a fine-looking man, though," said the banker's wife.

"He is not my ideal of manliness! I like men such as William Tell, powerful, plain and sterling; he has such a soft, dreamy expression in his face, at the same time such a superior, polite smile, and a pair of eyes which no one can make out; now they look as if they had disappeared; then again gleam diabolically, now small, now large; eyes, as to the nature of which no one can form a decision. Yet, I have read somewhere that girls like that. What success Don Juan had, mamma! His register that Leporello unrolls is longer than the *menu* at the largest hotel! But it is not that alone, believe me, mamma; it is being a nobleman! The influence which rank exercises upon love is very great! Those who have nothing particular about them, excepting being noblemen—and it does prepossess people—have married the most beautiful girls. How often have I not already said that papa ought to have himself ennobled! With his money and his connexions it would be a trifle; but you do absolutely nothing to smoothe my path through life—to assist me to success. Some portion would fall to your share, too; you would like to be *gnädige Frau*, and it is impossible to give that to oneself."

While Salomon told his troubles to his mother, and as he added would try his luck with Eva once more, another rival of Blanden's had arrived unexpectedly, and was present at this forest-party, the young poet Schöner, who for a short time at least had applied for a place in Eva's heart, and had striven to be successful in obtaining it. But since that encounter with the singer, Eva had renounced him so completely that she treated him with conspicuous coldness.

Had he not accompanied the admired *virtuoso*, on the whole of her tour, back to the capital, and only left her when she made a trip into the country with a female friend, to Lithuania or Masuren, and forbade the young poet to escort her farther?

Schöner easily recovered all these slights and resigned himself to the existing state of affairs; he hoped soon to reconquer the lost position; he sunned himself with such self-satisfaction in the glory of an easily-gained, doubtful fame, that he was less susceptible of smaller defeats.

In addition, his spirits, like his poetry, were still sparkling champagne, and a certain youthful unripeness did not become him badly; his nature owned tokens of genius which promised that he would overcome it.

Blanden, with that subtle discrimination which was peculiar to him, soon remarked that Eva's indifference did not appear to be at all natural in this case, that slight defiance, something repellant lay in it, indicating former connection. He looked more closely at his rival, who did not displease him at all, and in whose poetical attempts he had already been interested, and found remarkable consolation in the former's turned-down shirt-collar, and in his unpolished thorn stick. He considered the entire toilet hopeless for a matrimonial candidate, that the heart of an educated girl, who aims at a domestic hearth, could not possibly repose any confidence in such a wooer.

Yet love, which allows itself to be won by an enthusiast and a pair of glowing eyes—had it no chance in the game?

Schöner was so engrossed by the political paroxysm of that period, that this intoxicated idealism lent him most infectious enthusiasm. He acknowledged himself to be Herwegh's disciple, and when he recited that poet's verses, the beautiful, powerful voice in which he declaimed them, always called forth a kindred feeling in his listeners.

He recited with the enthusiasm with which, at that period, these poetical fire-brands were hurled into the air, and, at the same time, heat the oak-branches with his thorn-stick, until the leaves whirled to the ground.

"Have you seen him in person?" he asked Eva, and, as she replied in the negative, he continued, "I was present when the students greeted him; I was present at the entertainment in the Kneiphöf *Junkerhof*, when he declaimed his marvellously beautiful poem—

> '*Die Lerche war's nicht die Nachtigall,*
> *Erhebt euch vom Schlumnur der Sünden;*
> *Schon wollen die Feuer sich überall,*
> *Die heiligen Feuer, entzunden.*'[3]

And the old Justizrath, with his long, thin arms patted Herwegh on his shoulders, and addressed a warm speech to him, and any one who could saddle a Pegasus, mounted his poetical steed, in order to do honour to the poet. A new epoch has dawned for poetry. I know your charming book-shelves, Eva; there they stand in delicate bindings—the romancists, Uhland, Platen, and Rückert, and whatever their names may be; the later born masters of song, who followed our classical writers, but where the mere empty appearance of cultivation is not in question, there the reverence of quiet natures buries itself in the solitary enjoyment of the poets, and they are mostly women and girls who give themselves up to such enjoyment. How totally different it has become now! Not only youths, but grown-up men are enthusiastic about Herwegh's poetry, as it does not find its echo alone in the students' drinking parties, but also in official bureaux and counting-houses. Herwegh's journey through Germany was a regular triumphant course; he was *fêted* everywhere; the King granted him an audience, and treated him as an intellectual Great Power. Poetry is becoming a national affair again; the beautiful times of Greece are returning once more."

"And do you not fear," said Blanden, "that this infatuation will be followed by a long reaction? that poetry, by these strong measures which it must employ to act upon the masses, will dull its power, and a time of universal indifference to it ensue?"

"I do not fear that," replied Schöner, "the last poet will only depart from the world with the last man, as Anastasius Grün has sung so beautifully."

"Oh, yes, singers will not fail," interposed Blanden, "but the public! The gentlemen of the profession will not give way, but I can well imagine a time when political poetry will be followed by political prose, when the ideals are attained which the poet's enthusiasm has lauded. That which, until now, has been the home of poetry, the kingdom of silent feelings, will be more forsaken than ever now, because, in the noise of public life, people have become unaccustomed to it. Then the poets will only sing of politics; yet these will need no more poetry; they would treat of more tender subjects, yet these retreat before politics. All poetry will then appear to be materials for use in sickness, which, in the present critical period, we have cast off from us."

"I cannot take so black a view," replied Schöner. "I believe in the everlasting youth of the mind, in the immortality of the beautiful, of poetry, even though the poets die. Who could subscribe to a *monumentum aere perennius*? I even doubt if Herwegh will produce anything great; he is only a man of the Awakening, of the lyrical Initiative. There is no versatile productive nature in him; a dull fanaticism lies in him, which has been able to give utterance to the cry of distress of the people and time, but hardly commands a wealthier spiritual life, and no varied forms of art. One single enchanting poetical blossom, like the torch-thistle, and then the busy, creative power is exhausted. His dreamy brow, his dark eye promise much, and if genius did not live in him, how could he have composed such entrancing poetry? But a heavy spell, as it were, rests upon him, and too early fame is poison."

"You speak your own condemnation," said Eva, with cold flattery.

"Oh, no, my Fräulein! I rejoice that my poems have found some little echo; yet this modest recognition is far removed from the noisy, clamorous path of triumph of those happy ones, upon whose brows fresh laurels have been lowered. Lasting fame can only be won by serious work, and the glorious aim of a maturer life."

Eva was astonished at this modest confession, which made a favourable impression upon Blanden. The self-satisfaction of the young poet, who was a spoiled favourite in certain circles of society, certainly drew pleasant nourishment from the frequently extravagant recognition with which he met; but the inmost kernel of his nature was not absorbed by it; the impetus to future greater performances remained alive.

Eva and her companions had become separated from the party during this animated conversation. From several symptoms, Schöner perceived that a little romance was being enacted, of which he himself was not the hero. He remained untroubled at this neglect, and, with noble unselfishness and a poet's pleasure in a little love tale, which he might utilise himself for a newspaper, he left the field, under the pretence that he had promised a beautiful bouquet to the Kanzleirath's Minna, and he must gather it in the wood. He also had the satisfaction in so doing of giving them to understand he would not act the superfluous third person's part of chaperon at this *rendezvous* of two lovers, and guessed their wish to be alone.

They had arrived once more at the spot where Blanden had first greeted his campanula; the alders rustled in the evening wind, the stream whispered beneath the trees; above through the quivering boughs of the weeping willows the western sky poured its floods of gold.

"You know this young poet well?" asked Blanden.

"I have met and talked to him several times, he interests me; he possesses talent, intellect and attractive qualities, yet the want of steadiness in his nature and actions repelled me; everything in him is prompted by the whim of the moment."

"And you felt no liking for him?"

"Just a very little liking, I do not deny it; he paid me attentions, people remarked it, and often threw us together in society; it flattered me, as he was accounted the ornament and pride of those circles, and he gazed at me with fervid eyes as though he felt a deep passion for me, but he looked at all the world with the same eyes, and when I recognised that, he became indifferent to me."

"He has the eye and heart of a poet! Such a heart yearns to possess everything beautiful that it looks upon as its own heaven-bestowed property; it is dangerous and fatal to win a poet's evanescent passion—he only gives it durability in his works, not in his life. How many blossoms of beautiful emotions has Goethe plucked, as it were, in passing by; to how many women's hearts did his wanderings bring death, like the approach of the inapproachable. That does not suit us inferior mortals! And even if in the extravagance of youth, we do yield ourselves up to such poetical paroxysms, we must soon learn to control ourselves, for we not only leave desolate the lives of others, like that poet, but also our own, as we are unable to cast imperishable creations into the other scale."

Eva looked questioningly at him with her large eyes.

"Let us sit down upon the grassy mound, among the blue-bells, they ring in spring, perhaps also for me; it was here I found my campanula."

Eva stood hesitatingly; he drew her down beside himself upon the sward.

"The girl that asks for feelings fresh as morn, must reject the man—reject him decidedly—who, after abundant experiences in far-off lands, returns to his home. My life is an Odyssey. I have suffered many shipwrecks; many a Calypso has bound me in her fetters, yet no Penelope awaits the home-comer, he has first to seek her."

Eva did not venture to look up, and plucked the blue flowers while he continued—

"Yet what are whirlpools and ocean wonders, the magicians and nymphs of other days—what all the harsh and sweet dangers of those seas which Homer's sun has illuminated for evermore, compared with the shoals and abysses which menace the bold traveller of the present time? To-day there is no Odyssey in which a vein of Faust would not be concealed, a struggle to fathom the world and life. And how wonderfully at this great turning-point of the period in which we are born, all truths and all delusions play into one another! And while still at home I succumbed to these perils! I saw how the old faith clung convulsively to the standard of the world's renunciation, in that religious enthusiasm which then held its sway over me, I joined it; yet beauty, which we learn to despise, passion, which we should renounce by oath, gained the victory within me over that belief. They all played a daring game, I succumbed to it, and I was not the only one; it was the first great step astray in my life."

Eva had laid her flowers in her lap; she did not dare to look at him—not with her eyes' mute question.

"I speak to you in enigmas, and may they remain enigmas to you! What I have experienced in the world were adventures that were only wafted upon me like gossamer threads in the air, which we shake off again. Only once beneath Italy's soft sky, in the intoxicating breath of its perfumed plains, a spell held me enthralled for a short time; I thought to live through one of Boccaccio's novels; the charm of concealment from those at home remained assured to this dream-like meeting. Enough, I returned home, no tired, no bowed down man, but tired of the life that I had led, overwhelmed with dark recollections, resolved, instead of an unsteady wanderer through the universe, to become a citizen of my country and of the world, who works nobly and bravely; for this I require peace, and peace of mind is alone the ground upon which such good work nourishes."

"And it will flourish," cried Eva, with exalted animation, "cast all sadness, all depression far behind you! I cannot bear to see shadows suffuse your brow —your eyes close as if expiring! I would see you happy, quite happy, and your name honoured like those of the noblest patriots, a Stein and Schön!"

"That word shall never be forgotten by me," cried Blanden, "it finds an echo in my soul; it tells of perfect unanimity of feeling, and if there is a cabala in life, you have thrown open the page on which the magic sentence stands, which now governs my days. That is the noble ambition which animates me now, with which I would banish the evil spirits, yet, I repeat, that to attain it I need also ensured peace at home. Let us reverse the old fairy-tale—I am an enchanted prince—will you be the princess who loosens the unholy spell?"

Eva blushed deeply, and covered her face with her hands—the blue-bells had fallen from her lap.

"Will you dedicate your whole life to me, that mine may open to new, soft bloom beneath the light of your beautiful gentle eyes? Will you be a true guardian to me, that I may never lose sight of the glorious goal which I strive to reach? I know that I am asking much; you are to give up to me a young pure life, while mine has been already furrowed and torn by the wild streams of passion; but is it not an old question whether love consists more of happiness than sacrifice?"

"A sacrifice," cried Eva, springing up suddenly; "a sacrifice, which is the greatest happiness!"

"That word announces mine! Then you will adorn my life, my lovely campanula? You will belong to me, my glorious Eva, my redeemer!"

"I will," said she, not whispering shamedly, but in a transport of ecstacy; and he folded her in his arms and pressed the betrothal-kiss upon her lips.

"Thus be my past life extinguished by this moment," cried Blanden. "I feel as if, pursued by evil spirits, I entered the sanctuary of a bright temple, and all the gods smiled me a welcome. Sacred be this moment to us: the rustling trees, the parting orb of day be witness of our betrothal!"

And again he folded Eva to his heart; she returned his caress amid burning tears, by which the pent-up tumult of her passionate love found relief for itself. Blanden felt too happy; again and again he listened to the assurances of perfect love. They wandered some time longer by the stream in the evening's light, then unconcernedly returned to the party.

This want of confusion was indeed ruinous to Eva's character. The Kanzleiräthin explained to her daughter that she must break off her intimacy with Eva, as it was positively astounding what liberties that girl allowed herself. She had always seen that the Kalzow's bringing up was a very sad one, but had not expected that it would bear such ruinous fruits. Salomon suggested to his mother that they had not merely been catching butterflies and gathering flowers, but that the science of nature also possessed other interesting pages which could be studied. Rath and Räthin Kalzow rejoiced silently at the favourable course which this mutual fancy took; at the same time the Rath had some misgivings which occasionally worried him, so that his coughing fits overcame him.

"It is quite beautiful," said he, confidentially, several times to his Miranda, "that Eva has conquered him; but who says then that his intentions are serious? She is a poor, middle-class girl; he, a rich, noble landowner, and even although, according to the universal law of the country, nothing stands in the way of such a marriage, yet up to the present time he has made no such declaration. The girl is beautiful as her mother, my poor sister, was."

Miranda merely vouchsafed a contemptuous shrug of the shoulders in reply to this eulogium.

"Yet beauty," continued the Rath, while setting his cravat to rights, "may suffice for love, but not for marriage, and to one who has knocked about in the world so much as Blanden, one adventure more or less does not matter. In fact, Miranda, if we have allowed Eva to be talked about again all for nothing, it would cause me sleepless nights."

Nor could Miranda either really suppress a few slight doubts; she comforted herself, however, with the thought that Blanden would probably remove these doubts himself.

Then the Kanzleiräthin, who had just taken a turn with the banker's wife through the hazel bushes, holding a couple of nuts in her hand, came running, almost breathlessly, across the meadow to the married couple.

"What do I hear? Why, that is the same Blanden whose name was often mentioned at the time when the seraphic community was talked of? Surely, he was a member of it."

"The grass has grown over it long since," said the Regierungsrath, annoyed.

"Besides, there are many Blandens in the province," added the Räthin.

"But all marks of recognition point to this one! I must say though," continued the Kanzleiräthin, triumphantly, after having cracked a hazel nut with her seal-like protruding teeth, "that I should not like to entrust my daughter to a pupil of those saints, not even for a walk in the forest, because he might easily mistake it for Paradise."

And cracking the second hazel nut, she left the Kalzows with the joyful conviction that she had caused them great trouble by this communication. Indeed, the Regierungsrath was obliged to admit to himself that this sect had caused evil misfortune enough in families; he had occasionally heard Blanden's name mentioned at that time. But his wife repeated, consolingly—

"You may safely believe it is not the same Blanden; it will be some cousin of a collateral branch. It is only a piece of the Frau Kanzleiräthin's spite, because no one notices her Minna, whom she always plays out as an ace, without ever making a trick by it."

The family's anxiety was, however, augmented when Blanden announced that he must visit his estates for a short period; would then, however, return, and he hoped should still find them at the seaside. It would have seemed like desecration of his feelings to confide his love just yet to her parents; it was still quite impossible for him to connect Eva in his thoughts with that undignified parental couple. What was unavoidable should only be done when the betrothal ceremony could follow immediately. But he must return home, because he had to present himself to his electors as candidate. Eva parted from him with perfect, joyful confidence, and when her mother hazarded a sceptical remark, she replied—

"We will wait patiently; everything will turn out for the best."

And such a happy ray suffused her countenance, that Miranda said to her husband, as she placed his cravats in a drawer—

"The girl is sure of her affair; she must have reason to be so."

The Rath chuckled significantly, and passed no sleepless night.

CHAPTER VII.

THE ORDENSBURG.

It was late at night when Blanden's carriage, with its steaming horses, stopped before the castle door of Kulmitten.

The picture of the Holy Virgin, with the Child Christ in her arms, gleamed high above the portal in the moonlight. The remains of an old Ordensburg had been built into the castle, giving it an historically venerable appearance. The emblem of the Knights of the German Order, the cross with an eagle, was to be seen on all parts, and even greeted the new comers from the portal. The old belfry, well-preserved with its underground dungeons, rose upon a hill close to the shores of a large lake, which, with the wide belt of woods that surrounded it, extended far away in the moon's silvery light.

It would be easy to have imagined oneself in the solitude of primeval forests, had not the old stronghold reminded one that this place was no virgin soil, but that here the iron course of history had already held its sway, and claimed the victims of bloody conflicts.

Doctor Kuhl, who would not be deprived of guiding the foaming team, sprang down from the box, as he exclaimed—

"This seems to be quite an interesting old nest; why, surely the conversion of heathenish Prussia is relinquished here! Else you must begin with me."

Servants and steward had assembled in the castle's portal. Blanden had hardly descended, before grey-headed Olkewicz, a Masure, whose cradle had stood by the Lake Marggrabowa, assumed an important mien, so as to deliver his report of the most recent events. But Blanden at once perceived his faithful steward's intention, and arrested it—

"Not now, Olkewicz! it will be time enough to-morrow! The castle still stands upon the same spot—and that is the principal thing. For the rest, go to sleep children! It is late at night; only Friederich shall stay up, and look after my guest and me."

Friederich lighted them through the vaulted hall; the pillars cast shadows upon the stone flags of the floor, and upon the old castle's strong walls. They ascended a stone staircase; the table was laid in the dining-hall of the Order. It was a magnificent room; a granite column in the middle supported the radiated arch. Faded glass paintings were still visible in the windows. Blanden opened them; his gaze wandered out over the wide lake.

"You must excuse me for a short time," said Kuhl. "I am a species of Aquarius, and must greet my native element; I am impelled like the late unhappy Melusine. I must away into the water!"

"Now, at midnight?" asked Blanden.

"Until I have had a dip in the lake, I cannot feel myself at home here. See how it lures me with those glistening lights which play upon its surface. There are probably no syrens in the lake; if there had been any, they would most likely have died long ere this of *ennui*. Can one not dive into it anywhere from a balcony or gallery?"

"That even at midnight would create great sensation."

"Well, then, I will go to the bushes on the banks."

Blanden sat at the windows of the dining-hall, lost in dreams; he pondered how the old castle would gain new life. He asked himself what impression the magnificent view over the wide lake and the tall woods, most of which formed part of his possessions, would make upon Eva, when she first sat here by his side?

Far away his friend splashed in the waves, and swam ever farther out into the lake; a considerable time elapsed before he appeared at the midnight repast. Then he was lighted to his room by the old servant, who was himself dismissed to rest by Blanden.

The master of the castle was in a condition of strange excitement; he could not sleep. He took the candle, and walked through all the apartments to plan their future distribution, and to find out where Eva would be most comfortable.

He first entered his library; it was a magnificent apartment, the shelves, containing books, reached up to the ceiling. The newest poets and authors of Germany, bearing well-known names, were not missing. Blanden esteemed it to be his duty to buy their works—a duty towards literature, which but few of his equals recognised.

In addition to these he also possessed all the newest foreign classics, numberless political, historical and philosophical works. A division that occupied one entire wall, was filled with works of travel of all descriptions; on one spot he perceived a conspicuous gap; several volumes were missing— who could have borrowed them?

A stuffed royal tiger, which he himself had killed on the coast of

Coromandel, stood before the shelves; beside it several stuffed Asiatic birds, amongst them one of Paradise, whose splendid tail sparkled in the light of the lamp which Blanden held in his hand.

Then he imagined that a small piece of paper was placed in the rare bird's bill; it was no delusion, he seized the paper and read the following words, traced upon it in unfamiliar handwriting—

"The bird of Paradise, according to the legends of Eastern nations, has no feet; such a bird of Paradise is the happiness of love. It may not take a firm foothold upon earth, else its sparkling brilliancy, its Argus-eyed splendour, its Paradise will be lost to it."

Blanden was astonished. Who could have written these lines? How came they hither? Was it a warning which met him just when he was about to found a lasting happiness upon earth? Yet it was impossible—no one even knew of it as yet.

He examined the other birds, and even at last the royal tiger, whether they, perhaps, could belong to the race of speaking animals and were supplied with significant notes; but all these creatures preserved unoffending silence.

A lion's skin was extended as a rug before the library table, towards which Blanden stepped, and whereon he perceived three open volumes were lying; they were plainly those works of travel which were missing from the shelf, writings upon Italy. The opened chapters treated of Lago Maggiore; red roses lay between the pages.

Blanden almost started affrightedly at the spirit which, during his absence, had bewitched his castle. Who could know of that secret meeting on the Lago Maggiore?

The amber merchant, who pretended to have met him on the shores of that lake once, rose to his mind. Yet, the red roses and the very pregnant sentence could have no connection with that disagreeable companion.

Thoughtfully, Blanden examined the handwriting—it seemed to be that of some woman.

His study adjoined the library. A number of letters had been accumulated into a heap upon the writing-table. Blanden glanced hastily at the caligraphy of the addresses, most of which indicated letters containing business matters.

Beside them lay his album, its clasp stood open; he looked inside, and on the last page read the following verse in the same handwriting—

"Oh, bliss is but a fleeting dream,
While lasting longing ling'ring stays;
Oh, wise betimes 'tis to resign,
And yet our souls with sadness teem,
For by the side of bounteous days
Long years of want are left behind."

Here, too, all signature was missing; yet, must he not now complete it? Who but that mysterious beauty on the Lago Maggiore could have written these lines? But how in the world could she come to this most remote neighbourhood—and how inside this castle?

He should have liked best to have awoke the steward at once to obtain information; painful impatience, which he could not subdue, had taken possession of him. He went through the suite of freshly-furnished rooms. The masons and upholsterers had just completed their task; the newly-built wing of the castle was simply and comfortably arranged; while not a sign of that haunting spectre allowed itself to be seen.

He visited the guest chambers; they were all in the most perfect order. Only once Blanden started, as close by, in the night's silence, he heard a peculiar noise. In his excitement he had quite forgotten his guest; it was Doctor Kuhl, who, snoring loudly, slept the sleep of the righteous.

From the dining-hall, Blanden went to the chapel, which adjoined it. The former belonged to the Ordensburg, and was still well preserved. A portion of the glass paintings in the windows were dedicated to the Holy Virgin, a portion to the deeds of the Knights of the Order. One picture portrayed the latter's battle with the Poles; the Virgin hovered above it amid light clouds.

Up several steps arose a small altar; behind it a picture, which represented the elevation of Christ upon the cross. Upon the altar lay another paper, with the words: "Remember the little fisherman's church on Isola Bella!"

Now there was no longer any doubt; that Italian woman had appeared here in the Baltic country, by the remotest lakes of Masuren. She had been to his castle: was it ardent, longing, unconquerable passion, that had urged her to follow him hither? She alone could know of that meeting in the little fisherman's church.

The ghost had long since ceased to make an eerie impression upon Blanden; but the enchanting days and nights that he had passed on the Lago Maggiore, seemed to glow again in his soul; that intoxicating perfume of the South, that beautiful woman's picture that had appeared and vanished again so mysteriously, had bound his recollections as if with some sweet spell.

He gazed out upon the lake. How cold and lifeless it seemed to him; the moon sank behind the western woods; a chilly north wind had arisen in the middle of the summer's night, and swept over the freezing waves! How cold these scentless trees, in their immeasurable monotony!

Before his mind lay the glorious southern lake, in the magical light of the moon, with its islands, that seemed to float upon its waves; one island sent forth its orange perfumes to another; a delicious breeze was wafted through the night.

The cold glaciers of the distant Alpine passes might gleam in the moonlight on the horizon like steel-clad giants; they were only the sentinels who guarded the gates of this Paradise; here all was warm, enchanting life; shores and islands resounded with songs. It was Armida's magic-garden; and how seductive was she herself—that Armida, sparkling with soul and passion!

Blanden called himself to order; how unseemly these recollections appeared to him just now; but despite violent efforts to ward them off, they rose ever again and again.

Impatiently he awaited the morning; but just as the red dawn cast the first pale gleam into the lake he had fallen asleep from over-fatigue, and in the morning's tardy dreams he saw mysterious figures which touched all the contents of his castle, so that a wondrous radiancy streamed forth from them, and through all the rooms he followed a closely-veiled figure, with a magnolia wreath in its hair.

It was late in the morning when he was awoke by Doctor Kuhl, who had just come out of the lake.

Blanden believed he must have dreamed the evening before. In order to convince himself that it was a real occurrence, he once more undertook a tour through the apartments which on the previous evening had offered him such enigmas.

The notes, the album-verses remained unchanged in the light of the morning's sun, just as they had been in the lamp-light. Blanden summoned his steward.

"Who has been here during my absence?"

"I wanted yesterday, *gnädiger* Herr, to tell you," said old Olkewicz, while assuming a reproachful manner, "but you would not allow me to speak!"

"Then tell me now!"

"It was a few evenings since that two ladies on horseback, with flowing veils, stopped before the castle gate. Their visit was to you, they said, and the one declared herself to be an old acquaintance of the *gnädiger* Herr; but it appeared to me that they knew quite well you were not here; they begged for permission to see the castle. And as even princes' castles are thrown open to visitors, and ours being a very grand, renowned one, and does not disgrace us, I conducted them round all the apartments; they expressed their admiration of the dining-hall and the chapel, and the beautiful arrangement of the new rooms, thanked me pleasantly, and mounted their horses once more, in order to ride through the wood to the nearest little town. It had been a sultry day; a heavy storm rose above the lake, a violent tempest lashed the waves, before a quarter of an hour had elapsed since the riders left the castle-yard. The trees in the woods crashed; the birches and pines, blown down by the wind, can still give you a token of the hurricane's violence. I became anxious about the ladies, but it was not long before they dashed into the court again, and prayed for hospitable shelter until the storm should be appeased. Your honour will deem it right that I did not refuse them this shelter."

"Certainly, old Olkewicz, we are, indeed, no barbarians."

"The storm discharged itself with fearful fury, and it remained hanging above the trees, and stood firmly in the sky for a long time. And by the time it passed away, night had set in. What remained to me, but to extend the hospitality still farther? The *gnädiger* Herr was not at home; I could then, without hesitation, grant the ladies a night's quarters without the *gnädiger* Herr's character—"

"Do not be troubled about that, it is weather-proof!"

"But it is incredible what disturbance a couple of female beings cause in the best regulated establishment. I believe if a woman came into this house, all would be topsy-turvy."

"We will wait and see, old man! But what more happened?"

"I could not sleep! A couple of strange people thus in the house—just as if one's eyes are full of dust; one has no peace! For a long time I sat under the old oak in the park and watched how the lights went from one room to another, like will-o'-the-wisps, and when they actually shone out of the old chapel's glass windows an eerie sensation overcame me, and I thought of the ghosts that dwell in such old churches. Why in the world should they pry about? Did they seek something? I should have liked to ask them; but it would hardly have been proper, they had already bid me 'good-night,' and probably hung their riding dresses upon the chairs. At last it became dark; only the moonlight, which came forth from the dispersing stormy clouds, was reflected upon all the windows.

"I decided to retire to rest also," old Olkewicz continued his relation, "and made only one more round of the castle. There—God punish me!—stood a white form with unbound hair, above upon the gallery of the tower, and gleamed as brightly as if she had intercepted the whole moonlight. I did not stir! She stood a long—long time—and stared out at the lake, her arms crossed, and then, again, as if musing, she rested her head upon her arm, and it upon the balustrade. She must have been visible a long, long way off, and if all had not been still as death upon the lake the sailors must have been frightened at the ghost high up upon the tower."

"Then this lake, too, has found its Lorelei," said Blanden, softly to himself.

"Early on the following morning both disappeared, after cordial thanks and considerable gifts; I felt quite comfortable again, as though we had been released from some haunting spirit."

"And how did these ladies look?"

"Well, the ghostly apparition upon the tower was worth seeing; she looked like a queen; her carriage was commanding, her voice had a beautiful ring. Whether brown or blonde, I did not study her so accurately; all colours seemed to me to play about her, she confused me so, after I had seen her up there as a spirit. The other was little, and had nothing at all ghost-like about her. She seemed to be an attendant; she resembled our housemaid, Bertha; she had a pair of small blinking eyes, and something sly about her whole person."

"It is possible that it was some spirit that sought me out," said Blanden to himself.

"If your *gnädiger* is convinced of it," replied Olkewicz, "I shall not contradict it at all! at least in our neighbourhood there is no sort of woman-kind that could ever so remotely resemble that lady."

"Say nothing concerning this visit," said Blanden, "and desire my people also to maintain silence about it. Enough thereof. To-day, wines, provisions and delicacies will arrive from Königsberg, whence I have ordered them. Make all, preparations for a large dinner that I intend to give. Keep the Castle clean, get the guest's stables into order!"

"About the harvest, *gnädiger* Herr—"

"Agricultural matters another time! Whether the harvest be good or bad we cannot alter it. Rain and sunshine do their best—even although we have visited ever so many agricultural colleges."

Old Olkewicz held quite opposite views, and was least of all satisfied that the young master had done away with the rule of the rod which formerly was in vogue here; his theory was based upon the great principle that, in order to garner good corn, the people must first be more threshed than the corn afterwards; yet he ventured upon no objection.

Kuhl had listened silently to the discussion. "Then here we sit in an enchanted castle," cried he, "and adventures seek you!"

"I must confess to you," said Blanden, "that I know no solution of this enigma. Certainly I entertain no doubt that it is yonder mysterious beauty who made me look upon Lago Maggiore in a doubly entrancing light; but how she found her way to the most remote of Masuren's lakes is inexplicable to me; and if no other feeling, curiosity at least urges me most pressingly to interest myself in her again."

"And may a poor mortal, then, whose path such charming adventures do not cross, not learn what the circumstances of the case are?"

"That you shall—and on this evening. I feel a need myself to bring those days once more before my mind. Yet to do so I need leisure and quiet, which the day's bustle will not permit. Look, there comes Wegen in his one-horse trap, he brings us news how matters look amongst the Phœacians."

His lively friend came in briskly and eagerly, a cigar in his mouth.

"These wind-falls in your forest—colossal! Trees lie about like toothpicks which have fallen out of an overturned case. The storm has even played havoc with an old oak yonder upon the dam, and hurled its head to the ground, as my Friederich does the plume of feathers on his hat, when I decline some entertainment; but how are you going on?"

"Blanden has had wonderful dreams," said Kuhl.

"Nothing new, nothing new," replied Wegen, stroking his moustache, "that occurs nightly with me. Friederich says it arises from the grey peas which I am passionately fond of eating in an evening; a man feels like an East Prussian when he sees such a dish before him. Lately I dreamed I was manœuvring with the Landwehr; I had to lead a company of sharpshooters. The signal sounds; my company stands like a wall; I rush furiously upon it; the fellows stick together and I cannot tear them asunder, give myself what trouble I may. The colonel rides up—'Thunder and lightning! Wegen, what are you doing?' and I awake bathed in perspiration! Horrible dreams! But even waking one does not meet with anything pleasant."

"What has happened, then?" asked Blanden.

"Well, Schön has fallen into disgrace; he relinquishes his post; the enemies of the constitution in Berlin bear away the victory."

"They do not want a constitutional State," interrupted Kuhl, "and even if

81

you did carry it through, it would only be the semblance. The State's machinery would become rather more complicated and expensive, and that is not desired; beyond that, they know quite well, that little else in the matter will be altered. What could otherwise be set in motion with one shove, would then require several handles and winches, in order to let a noisy parliamentary machinery play; majorities are needed, and when things are needed, there they are too; more intelligent ministers are required—that is all! At present their signatures impose upon people, then their personal qualities must do so; but if you think that anything else will ever be carried out than what the Government chooses, it is a great mistake. Much dust will be raised, then those who would fain be great in Parliament would come and cry, 'I have raised all that dust,' like the fly in the fable. The car of the State, however, would roll on its way amidst the dust, and in that direction too, in which it is guided. *Timeo Danaos et dona ferentes!* A constitution would be a Danaîdes gift to Prussia!"

"No," replied Blanden, "that which Schön and others of the same mind have been preparing for a long time, will only prove beneficial for this country when it gains life. That is my firm conviction; free constitutional forms would bring another spirit into the people. While we who demand a constitution are now deemed to be rebels, a time will come, when the most zealous bureaucrats will look upon such an organisation as the most natural, and will not comprehend how any one could ever doubt it, or rather have quite forgotten that the courage and zeal of the East Prussian communities first unfurled this banner. But the obstinate refusal of the Government in Berlin fills me with joyful courage for the fight. How does it stand with my guests, Wegen? Have you seen about my invitations?"

"Well," said Wegen, as he stroked his moustache, much satisfied, "I have managed my affair well; they are all coming, all. Some out of politeness, others from motives of political zeal and a sense of duty, as they would know, of course, what a candidate for election has to say to them; many from curiosity, to become acquainted with the Ordensburg. They did not find you at home on their return visits; in short, you will have a perfect rainbow of political colours at your table; naturally all the others very pale, the liberal red outshining them. But, my dear friend, I have still to go to the district town. The Landrath is from home for a few days; he returns to-morrow, and will not be missing from your dinner; the Chief Deputy of the district has gout, so I must represent him. Look at me; to-day you see in me the Father of the district; do you not perceive the dignity of my demeanour? Even a couple of legal document wrinkles have put in their appearance! But I find nothing prepared for my reception. I do not mean wooden, triumphal arches, nor unattractive maidens clad in white, but something palatable—an enjoyable breakfast."

Blanden took care that a breakfast should be served, by which Wegen did his duty bravely, and then conducted his friend, at the latter's desire, to the stables. They were splendid places; Blanden had been as careful that horses of the finest race should fill his stalls, as he had been in devoting the most anxious attention to the neglected breed of sheep in East Prussia. He showed this living inventory, not without contented pride, and Wegen, in his good nature, went so far as to indulge this little weakness of his friend, and to let himself be led again and again into the agricultural sanctum, although he already knew every horse's head so accurately that he could have sketched it, and had sorted the wool of each single sheep on its body.

Then together they looked at the new buildings which Wegen had especially superintended, because Blanden, from horror of the masons' noise, had taken flight.

"The guest-chambers have been carried out according to your plans," said Wegen, "but I permitted myself to have them ornamented with a few elegant additions. It is too cruel the way guests are treated in most houses; one is shoved into a bare room, a sort of guard room, in any corner of the house, like an old travelling trunk or carpet-bag. These elegant canopied beds and carpets, the toilet-table furnished with everything that Parisian genius has invented; even upon the chest of drawers, work materials with needles, upon the little tables beside the beds, the newest German and French novels for reading before going to sleep, are my idea. Certainly it costs a fearful sum, and in addition of your money; but you will be satisfied with it, as Kulmitten will be a radiant example for all East Prussia, and what is done for civilisation is never lost."

Blanden nodded pleasantly and approvingly to his friend, who was chatting in the brightest wine-inspired mood, and then accompanied him to his carriage, in which he drove away to occupy the proud place upon the *sella curulis* of a Prussian Landrath.

As the evening's twilight had crept in, Blanden with Doctor Kuhl sat upon the balcony of the castle, looking over the lake. It was a cool summer evening; heavy leaden clouds lay above the lake, and the tall oak trees which shut in its broad mirror—there must have been thunder in the distance; the remains of stormy clouds were thrown up one above another, like charred logs of wood, and a freezing blast swept over the lonely lake. The lamps beside which Blanden and his friend sat, trembled in the soft sway of the evening breeze; the whole effect of the landscape had something mournfully wearisome, disconsolately monotonous; behind it again lay woods and lakes, lakes and woods; the course of cultivation had hardly touched these districts;

the life of the people, the life of individuals pointed to but few memories in these forsaken places. Before Blanden's mind arose, with double charm, the picture of that Italian landscape, where in one paradise of nature, taste and cultivation create themselves enchanting asylums, where every foot's breadth of land stirs up fascinating recollections, and has been overcome by civilisation, where the great pilgrim train of strangers brings the culture of Europe in ever changing forms.

Under the influence of this mood, he began to relate his adventure on Lago Maggiore to his friend.

CHAPTER VIII.

ON LAGO MAGGIORE.

"Any one who reads one of those older Italian romances, feels himself irresistibly attracted by the free breath of adventure which pervades it; I know, indeed, that in our respectable society where every one carries his passport in his pocket book, this adventuresomeness cannot find a place; it is proscribed, and I do not see either how it can be otherwise in our condition as citizens.

"All the same, it meets the untrammelled wanderer here and there; it wears a mask before its face, but it gazes fiercely and seductively through that mask.

"I have often meditated as to wherein the charm of those fleeting meetings consists, which in no case lay claim to any endurance; it is the charm of freedom and want of fetters. There is something oppressive to the mind in this consciousness of durability, in order to reconcile oneself to it deeper reflections are needed about the necessity that fetters man's life, and the pride of a sense of duty reconciles us to the constraint of the unalterable.

"But adventure arouses affections and feelings, and touches strings, which are sure to exist in human nature; never does the blood flow more lightly and freely through our veins; never does our mental life develop more ozone than in these tempests of passion, quickly as they pass away again in the sky. Also, if that enduring bond and that nobility of feeling is wanting, which only true love of the soul is capable of giving, yet something remains that ennobles the fleeting transport of passion, the rapture about beauty which is so closely united to love, but which has paled and must be repudiated in our circumstances.

"But where do these homes of adventure lie more than in the masked land of Italy? Are we not thrilled with those spirits of revelry which in the Venetian Carnival of that glorious *maestro* spring and dance upon the strings, and seem to be beside themselves in wild exhilaration?

"Here upon the Rialto, there upon the market place, mysterious glances beckon to us, seductive pressure of the hand invites us. This is a proud beauty of the people, who at other times wears the *fazzoletto*, that is a lady of position who seeks a *cicisbeo*. And upon the Roman Corso, when the long row of carriages drives down the street, we stand upon the carriage step and a delicate hand presses a bouquet into ours. Here adventure has risen and increased until it became crime, and gazed ominously and fatally at us out of the soft eyes of a Lucrezia Borgia and a Beatrice Cenci.

"But what heaven also in the land of Boccaccio, what rapture in the air, what charm in the aroma of the perfumes, which are set free by the day's glowing sun, which the evening's breeze wafts over the meadows, above the marble floors in the villas and in their sleeping chambers! There one must be a pedant, like the man from Arpinum, to think and to write of duty in a Tusculum; we other men follow Horace's example, wreath our heads with roses, take a wine bowl in our hands, and a beautiful Lydia in our arms.

"Enjoy the moment! Thus preaches Hesperia, and he who wreathes himself with its wildly growing myrtles does not remember the myrtle of German hot-houses, with which the bride adorns herself for life. I know Florence, that city of flowers, Rome the city of ruins; noisy Naples, where the tide of men, and the beating of the ocean's waves blend their roar, and whose single cyclopean eye is fire-belching Vesuvius. Yet nowhere did I feel so much at home as on the upper Italian lakes; and in spite of all the charms of Lago di Como, that splendid divided radiant mirror, which is most beautiful at that point whence one can overlook both its separate arms of water which twine themselves around the villa-clad heights; despite the loveliness of Lago di Garda, and its northerly port, above all others I have enshrined Lago Maggiore in my heart and spent two years of my life upon its shores. I know all the Swiss and Italian towns on its borders; but I lingered most fondly in Stresa, because from it a quick passage by boat bore me to the jewels of the lake, the Boromean islands.

"It was one beautiful summer's evening that I stood upon the topmost terrace of the Isola Bella; the lake glistened in the evening's crimson splendour; varied lights danced in the winding cypress walks, in the concealed shell-grottoes, and played upon the statues and obelisks of the uppermost terrace. The sister isles, the towns on the shores, the vine-surrounded villa-clad hills lay on the opposite side in a softer sheen. Sasso Ferrato, with its rocky walls, rose up defiantly in the lake; as if bathed in a red-hot glow, stood the ice-armour of the snowy peaks which guard the Alpine passes, which here lead down to the lake of Geneva, yonder to that of the four Cantons. Picturesquely the fiery red of the sinking sun contrasted with the glorious green of the Lago.

"How often people have blamed the *baroque* taste, the green *roccoco* of this Isola Bella! And yet, why should one not place a jewel in a brilliant artistic setting? This Isola Bella is the most beautiful belvidere on the lake; why should that belvidere not be splendidly decorated? The art which is lavished upon that small spot of earth does not detract from that vast nature which encloses it with her gigantic Alps! And then there is something soothing in these hiding places amongst the trees, these shell-grottoes—they invite one to quiet talk, to silent happiness; and how full is the heart, when the magic of this glorious nature, these evening lights, those perfumes flowing from a hundred flower calex—the whole of that fervidly-breathing life has inspired us!

"As I stood upon the terrace, lost in dreams, two ladies appeared, accompanied by a servant in livery, who remained standing close beneath the unicorn, the arms of the Boromei; they were both tall slender figures of distinguished appearance. I bowed politely and addressed them; one was able to speak German, and the circumstance that we could thus converse without being understood by her companion, soon gave us the semblance of a certain intimacy; her whole manner was animated; she treated every subject of conversation with great vivacity, she expressed the most supreme admiration for the beauties of the scenery, in doing which, however, she preferred to employ Italian exclamations and expressions, and Tasso's language sounded so mellow, so mellifluous from her lips that I listened with silent satisfaction to that melody as if to an artistic treat.

"I looked more closely at her; she was a beautiful woman. The nobility of her features was in harmony with that magnificent form; the sculptors' and painters' ideals in the Academy and Pitti Palace of the city of flowers seemed to have gained life in her. Everything within me cried: that is beauty, such as is fitting for this enchanted garden; thus must the queen of these isles, these waves have been! And it appeared to me as if the evening's crimson, which flowed down the tall figure, and then glided into the waves, was a glorifying effulgence shed forth from her. She dazzled and enchained me; I also soon remarked that her words, looks, countenance, told of the perfect sympathy with which I inspired her.

"The other lady was distant and reserved; her demeanour was that of a proud princess. As she took her departure, she dismissed me as it were with a slight bow; but in her companion's eyes I read something like the hope of meeting again.

"I would not disappoint this hope, and daily, at sunset, found myself on the terrace of Isola Bella. Two evenings I waited in vain; but how great was my joyful surprise when, on the third evening, I met her, and, indeed, quite alone. I welcomed her with a heartfelt and warmly returned pressure of the hand.

"'My friend has left,' said she, soon after the first exchange of greetings; I learned that she now lived quite by herself in a villa at Stresa. Our conversation became lively, but it avoided everything personal. She knew Germany and German affairs, but her enthusiasm was all for beautiful Italy, where Art and Nature both disclose themselves in such enrapturing beauty. We spoke of poets, painters, theatres and music. The sun had disappeared behind the hills; only its reflection still hung upon the rosy-tinted western clouds, but to-day the scene on the terrace was peculiarly animated. Countless miladies, with red guide-books, and guttural-voiced milords succeeded one another; they cast a few cursory glances at the lake, convinced themselves that all the guaranteed items of its decorations stood on their proper places, as they are described in books—here, the Isola Madre and del Pescatore, there the Sasso Ferrato, here Stresa, yonder Pallanza—and finally took leave with an expression of perfect satisfaction. Then came a few noisy Frenchmen and women, who uttered their delight on finding a morsel of Versailles in this Italian water-basin, and then sought the laurel tree in which Napoleon had cut the word '*battaglia*' before the battle of Marengo.

"It was a restless coming and going! As if in silent accord, we turned our steps towards the lonely shaded walks of the evergreen island, beneath the pines and cypresses, laurels and camellia trees. We did not talk much; often we walked silently side by side. The dusk of evening and of the green leaves seemed to hold us chained in some sweet spell. When we spoke, we spoke of that which was nearest to us, which stirred our feelings, of Nature's charms and the splendour of the manifold southern plants which were assembled there like a green court-dress for the old Palazzos; nor were the northern fir trees wanting, and I remarked that they reminded me of my home. Yet she asked no more about it. It was like a secret understanding between us not to disturb our mutual *incognito*, and thus even to envelop the circumstances of our lives in the same charm of twilight as that which hovered over the enchanted island.

"We descended the steps of the palazzo to the shore; an elegant gondola, with a gondolier in livery, was awaiting them.

"'May I invite you,' asked she, 'to accompany me in my bark as far as Stresa?'

"I accepted this invitation with pleasure.

"The moon had risen; the mountains' shadows floated in the silvery waves. The skiff drew a broad furrow in the molten silver that seemed to drip from the oars; the pines by the villas on the shore intercepted the moonlight with their broad fans. Like a sparkling plateau the glaciers of the Simplon Pass gleamed above a little cloud.

"How many magnificent villas shone beneath intensely dark, silvered green on the shores! Which was hers? I did not venture to ask, and she did not point to the spot on which she had taken up her abode.

"We stand under so many influences of culture, that not only our thoughts, but also our feelings, are regulated by it. That which great poets have described, bears for us the significance of personal experience; it is just as vivid in our imagination. Shakespeare's characters, which he received from Italian novels, stood before my fancy. Not a Julia was my companion, but she reminded me much of Portia; was not this the same moonlight glamour that hovered around the Belmont Villa? She possessed the figure and demeanour of a much-courted, aristocratic lady, the spirit and fervour of that enterprising rich heiress: where was her Villa Belmont? In her presence, I stood beneath the magic spell of Shakespearean poetry.

"At Stresa, I went on shore; her skiff was rowed still farther on. She vanished like a beautiful dream in the twilight of the moon's illumination that in the shrubs on the shore mingled with the shadowed mirror of the waters.

"For three evenings in succession I returned to the Isola Bella, and on each evening I found the mysterious beauty there. This adventure had gay shimmering butterfly's wings; I could not brush the coloured down from them. Naturally, liking and intimacy grew out of this constant intercourse; I hazarded bolder expression of the same. I praised her as my Armida, who held me within her spell; I praised the greater bliss that Rinaldo had enjoyed. She did not turn aside; she looked at me with her luminous eyes, as though she would read deeply in my soul. Then she sighed, plucked a camellia which bloomed beside us, and pulled it musingly to pieces.

"As we traversed the little fishing harbour of the island, in order to enter our gondola for the homeward journey, we perceived that a heavy storm was coming toward us from the Simplon, and with increasing rapidity was darkening the lake. Its billows surged uneasily, and the forks of lightning broke in the disturbed mirror of the waves. The return passage was impossible; where should we wait until the storm was over?

"'I know a comfortable place of refuge,' said she; 'here, the little fisherman's chapel. It is, as a rule, lifeless and deserted; the fishermen only pray there when they go out to fish. It is the Madonna of eels and salmon-trout who protects that sanctuary.'

"We entered the little church; all was still and pleasant there. Outside the tempest raged, and the thunder rolled with such might that the building rocked on its foundations.

"Italian churches are accustomed to be used as asylums of love. Protestant churches would be desecrated by every love which does not come before the altar; the Madonna's eye rests without anger upon the bliss of lovers exchanging vows.

"Indeed, it was only a delusion of my senses when I believed she cast an angry glance upon me, while I held my beautiful companion firmly, and pressed a fervid kiss upon her lips; it was only a sudden flash of lightning that quivered over the altar-picture.

"The glorious woman whom I encircled with my arms, was just as little wrath as the Madonna.

"And yet—is it not temerity of the man who only ventures to offer to the woman transient love? Has she not the right to a love that shall fill his whole life? May he without awe, without the fear of conscience, touch this holy thing?

"I was intoxicated by the moment; I did not think of the future. I accepted nothing, I declined nothing, but the *gens d'arme* who dwells in our bosom, to whom I had not listened for so long, asserted himself. I felt, in spite of all, in the presence of those fiery kisses, something of a subject's duty. I mentioned my name, position and place of habitation.

"But she laid her hand, as if imploringly, upon my lips—

"'Not these confessions, which I shall not, cannot return; shall we, then, frighten away the present beautiful dream? The witchery of happiness lies in mystery. You must never learn my name! Give me your word never to try to discover it.'

"I promised; but demanded urgently that her whole heart should be mine. She looked wondrously beautiful in the darkened chapel, when a ray of lightning, illumining her fine features, seemed to trace her figure in dazzling outlines in the twilight.

"'I only remain here three more days; then I disappear for ever—'from you also.'

"'Three days—well, but three days of perfect happiness may atone for everlasting separation. Three days—but they must be three days that can never be forgotten. Let us not think of the cold duty that constrains us to part, let us but remember that three days are still before us—yet I do not even know your name!'

"'Call me Giulia; it is one of the names that I bear.'

"In crash upon crash the storm discharged itself above us; more tempestuous became my vows. She bent towards me, whispering—

"'Men think but lightly of a heart that is quickly won, and are ever ready to repay fond love with forgetfulness and contempt.'

"I protested that that would never be the case with me.

"'And I asseverate that my heart never yet was weak enough to cherish a love which could have no hope of being a part of my life. I have struggled against love in sleepless nights, but it seemed to me as if the genius of my life rose up erectly and distinctly before me, and said—'If into your poor ruined life a sunny ray of happiness should fall, oh, then, open all your windows to it! And if it be only a short gleam of light that soon passes away, yet it will remain in your soul, full of consolation for the gloom into which the coming night plunges you. If misfortune be solemnly decreed to you by heaven and earth, if it hold you in an indissoluble spell, oh, then have courage to grasp happiness yourself; grasp that which heaven and earth would deny you. But intense love is bliss, bliss unutterable; its intensity is not measured by its lastingness—the moment is its watchword. In your arms, from your kisses I have felt what, until now, life could never give me; what only as the dream of the supreme was quickened in my soul. To every human being is granted one supreme moment—once birth and death—once the bliss of perfect love!'"

"'My Giulia!' cried I, deeply stirred by her fervour.

"'Never, never can I be yours!' cried she, 'but we will meet again to say farewell! I live in the Princess Dolgia's villa! This evening come to the pavilion; here is the garden key. No one will see you; at that hour all is deserted, the Princess herself is from home; only few servants are left at the villa.'

"I kissed her lips and hands in wild devotion.

"The tempest, meanwhile, had receded farther down the lake; the moon stood amid the broken clouds, which raced in wild career around the summits of the Alps. Our bark glided softly over the now bright, now dark waves. This time Giulia showed me her villa. It was a splendid building, buried amongst flowers; it shone brightly in the moonlight.

"'There, on the left, is the pavilion,' said Giulia, as she designated a Turkish kiosque. Laurels and myrtles surrounded it; a red fir, also, from the far north, lent its shade.

"As we stepped on land, a man came out of the bushes on the shore, close to Giulia. I could not recognise his features; they were half enveloped in a kerchief.

"Annoyed at this obtrusion, I was about to send him away, but she restrained my interference with a slight movement of the hand. He spoke vehemently to her in Italian, but, in an to me, incomprehensible dialect. His gestures were somewhat menacing, so that I held myself in readiness to come to the assistance of my beloved one; but he withdrew quietly, apparently satisfied with Giulia's replies.

"She looked pale as she held out her hand, bidding me farewell for a short time.

"All my spirits were in a state of ebullition. I ascended the heights behind Stresa. I was impelled along a pathless course through vineyards and chestnut groves; the sky was again overcast. Gloomily lay the surface of the lake, but it was as though, beneath the covering of clouds, a hotter breath brooded over the earth.

"I inhaled deep draughts of the burning air of that voluptuous nature—my pulses were at fever height.

"At the same time I was possessed with a sick dread of losing the key, and every moment I felt if it were still in my pocket.

"The evening hour struck from the church tower of the little town on the shore. For half-an-hour already I had been wandering round the villa, in which no lights were shining.

"The marble balustrades and pillars gazed gloomily into the cloudy night, but the air was perfumed with a hundred invisible flowers.

"Then something like a will-o'-the-wisp quivered in the pavilion! a little lamp illuminated the branches of the red fir-tree which kept guard before it. I opened the garden door and entered the leafy walks.

"She was waiting for me at the entrance of the dainty little round building. Mats covered the floor; ottomans with soft cushions were spread round the walls, which higher up were wreathed with garlands of flowers.

"The air wafted an exquisite perfume inside and through the open window.

"She appeared more beautiful to me than ever; she was a night-flower, created for night and moonlight. Her complexion was of that *morbidezza* of the Venetian women, which lends them such a melancholy charm; and by day, too, she wore her hair in the artistic manner of the Venetians, plaited at the side, behind a daintily-coiled head-dress. But now it flowed in dark abundance over the yellow shimmering moiré dress. She received me sadly: was not the coming parting hovering over our bliss of the present moment as restless foreboding hovers over every happiness?

"I have often read in books written by those who are learned in art, that all beauty is a self-sufficing copy of the eternal idea, whose enjoyment alone can grant harmonious contentment, that its reign ceases when the will's emotion desecrates its impalpable glory.

"It is heresy to think otherwise about it, and yet I do think otherwise. Even that people of god-like beauty, the Hellenes, thought otherwise, else they would never have invented the legend of Pygmalion: that is the solution of the enigma—beauty which does not only satisfy the ideal senses, which overpowers the whole man, so that without volition he is seized by its magic power.

"Amongst the Lemures of the East Prussian exorcists, woman, in her magical power, had first crossed my path; and that spirit of adoration which so long had held me in its bondage, was vanquished for evermore.

"Here, beneath Italy's laurels and myrtles, I was Pygmalion; but it was no cold marble that I folded in my arms. Was I ever a poet, I was one then; hymns of rapture flowed through my soul.

"For three evenings I was permitted to visit her; on the third the full moon stood above the red fir tree. The cracking of its branches in the night wind reminded me of my distant home.

"We wandered silently in the garden, forgetful of time—of everything—but that the oppression of the parting hour weighed upon us. She must go; she repeated it; I did not ask her why—I asked nothing. I still stood beneath the whole magic of her presence. Morning dawned at last, and released the dark masses of the groups of trees from the darkness with which they had been blended.

"It was a morning full of mournful sadness; tears hung on Giulia's long eye-lashes.

"'Let your thoughts return to these days, these happy days, as to a fairy-tale—for me they were more, far more! They have quite effaced all the rest of my life; and yet I must return to joyless gloom. I must—and, therefore—farewell!'

"One more burning kiss, one last embrace; I felt her tears upon my cheeks; her locks flowed over me like a tide of endless pain—we parted!

"After the little garden door was shut, something rustled near me amongst the shrubs, beneath the chestnuts; as I went farther on, I perceived a figure creeping behind me, which reminded me of that singular stranger who had already once played the spy upon us on the shore; however, I did not trouble myself about him, but went to my hotel, without again looking behind me.

"I kept my promise faithfully not to enquire about this queen of the night who had bloomed for me in such enrapturing splendour on the banks of that magic lake; held to it so faithfully that for a long time I avoided asking myself who that mysterious beauty could be?

"There is a heart's shrine for relics which one may not touch without destroying the charm that clings to those sacred recollections—the lotos-flower, which is the cradle of a god no hand may touch.

"Never to be forgotten are the days and nights on the shores of that beautiful lake. I have seen lakes in the highlands of Mongolia, amongst the mountain-giants of Thibet; but all these pictures were effaced beside the burning outlines in which the Lago Maggiore printed itself upon my soul.

"All the same in later times I often surprised myself in reprehensible curiosity; who was this Lady of the Lake? Her highly-bred manner told that she was a lady of distinction—an equal of her friend, that princess, in whose society I had first seen her. But the fetter that bound her? Was it the bond of matrimony, for which, however, in Italy, in the most aristocratic circles, the *cicisbeat* offers a compensation, rendered sacred by custom!

"I thought of the Countess Guiccioli, Byron's beautiful beloved—she did not conceal her happiness from her husband—and tie used to drive his favoured rival out in Ravenna, in his carriage and six—yes, the former rented quarters in the Count's castle.

"The secret that my Giulia preserved so fearfully must be of another kind. Perhaps she was being persecuted—politically persecuted; there are highly-born women enough in Italy, who stand upon the list of the proscribed; and if she never spoke of politics it was, perhaps, in order to avert all such thoughts from me. In this way, too, it would be easiest to explain the appearance of that obnoxious stranger, who surely was a subordinate agent of her political party.

"Certainly, I always asked myself again and again, whether love which withholds every confession excepting that of its own existence, which veils everything excepting its own intensity, is not an error? Love requires the whole man to be pledged, and may not appear with a mask, such as the Parisian ladies of simplicity carry before their faces. Otherwise it is but an adventure, and as an entrancing adventure I preserve that meeting in my memory; but I am weary of adventures, they have seduced me long enough, rendered my life disturbed and unsteady; precipitated my soul from one intoxication into another, but at last, after all, only left internal desolation behind.

"And now this mysterious Giulia appears suddenly here, in my castle. Has she given up her secret—does a duty no longer bind her to maintain it? Has a turning-point in the circumstances of her life been attained? What brings her hither?—only love for me? My name, my place of abode, she knew—she has noted it better than I believed, as she seemed too indifferent to listen to it; but what does she seek here—what can she bring me but disappointment? The glamour of the magic-lantern is burned down; here are no evergreen islands, no myrtles and laurels—and a Venus Aphrodite would shiver with cold, if she had to rise out of these chilly waters.

"To all these questions, which shall no longer disquiet me, I have the answer ready—my betrothal to Eva Kalzow—and this I will hasten, in order to oppose a decided fact as a defence against the adventure which seeks me here. I have broken with my past, and I will not that what is past should interfere any longer with my present life."

Blanden had finished his recital; Doctor Kuhl, who had listened attentively, let the cigar in his hand die slowly out, as, after a rather long silence, he began to hum a popular air.

"And you say absolutely nothing?" Blanden enquired of his friend.

"I think," replied Kuhl, "a *principessa* always remains a *principessa*—a Venus a Venus—in the North as in the South; I should have her turned out at the first opportunity, by your friend the Landrath, if she let herself be seen again in this district. She is a sort of beautiful pagan goddess—a sort of Bride of Corinth—and these ghosts are dangerous, especially for brides who are not so very distant, and whom the clergyman shall bless. But it has become late! One more dip in the sea, and then I will dream of your marble bride!"

CHAPTER IX.

AN ELECTION DINNER.

The Ordensburg Kulmitten had donned a festive garb; its portal was garlanded with flowers, the servants appeared in livery, and the Jäger's plume of feathers especially attracted the hall-boys' and dairy-maids' attention when he showed himself in the doorway.

Towards noon the carriages containing the guests arrived. Wegen was the first; he had decorated himself with the cross of the Order of St. John, which also adorned Blanden's breast.

Wegen immediately rushed about like a whirlwind over the whole house! even the cook in the kitchen had to doff his white cap to him. There he was a person to be respected; he knew many secrets of the culinary art, and conversed with the cook like one who understood the dishes whose names stood upon the *menus*, and also those which ought to have stood there. Then he went with Olkewicz into the wine-cellar, and had bottles with the most divers labels upon them marshalled upstairs, like regiments before a battle.

"This is no ordinary dinner, good Olkewicz," said he, while deciding upon the order of battle. "To-day we aim at gaining votes, and for that purpose these here are our best coadjutors. Here sherry and Madeira, which put people into a good humour, so that they become most susceptible of farther enjoyments; there good claret—people thaw, conversation begins, the political arena is opened; opposite opinions greet one another politely, like combatants with their rapiers. There delicious Rhenish wine, Metternich'scher Johannisberger, flowers of the reaction; things become more lively already; the debate grows animated, sympathies find one another out, those of the same opinions shake hands together, opponents exchange fiery glances, and fight hand-to-hand. Political pulses beat high. Then comes Widow Cliquot, and, by magic, sheds a rosy light all around her; a conciliatory spirit prevails; people only feel that they are patriots, citizens of the Prussian Fatherland; even enemies now shake hands.

"That is the moment; when the reserve champagne bottles are uncorked, then must Blanden, too, overflow, with a right delicious, foaming, sparkling speech; then all goes merrily; enthusiastic consent; chairs are pushed aside; the election is ensured, and a few glasses of Tokay guard against any weak termination of the meeting. Well, then, here stand our auxiliaries—a gay army, with all possible caps—and in any case very numerous; that is the principal thing!

"On that point I agree with Napoleon—victories only are gained by numerical preponderance."

When Wegen returned to the reception room from the kitchen and cellar, he found that as yet Herman, of Gutsköhnen, and Sengen, of Lärchen, were the only guests present. They were the squires of small manors, to whom a frock-coat was an uncomfortable acquisition; they wore blue habiliments with steel buttons, and looked in amazement at their reflections in the great pier glasses of the Kulmitten drawing rooms. They were adherents of Blanden, whose hand they shook heartily; was the latter not a cavalier, not merely in political, but also in social respects? Doctor Kuhl felt himself especially drawn to them; their Herculean figures attracted him, as did the deficiency of a frock coat, for his own in which he had passed his doctor's examination had long since been hung in the lumber closet; in politics, also, he loved the representatives of the ancient cantons, the powerful men of the people, and commenced a conversation with them which, beginning with the yoking of oxen, ended with the democracy of the future.

"We must first elect worthy representatives like Blanden," said he, for he considered that he owed this acknowledgment to his friend, "but that is only the beginning. Our aim is a constitution, in which every member of the State can record his own vote upon every question. Can any one be actually represented? As little in politics as in love. Such a deputy seems to me like a harlequin, who is patched up out of so many voting papers; if he chatters about freely with a speaking trumpet, he is applauded and admired; yet he still merely represents his own views and his own convictions; there are many questions springing up afresh, upon which I myself may take a different view. What use is it to me? When I have once given my vote, from a political point of view, I am a squeezed out lemon, a cypher. Every man should give his own vote for his own opinion on every question; so must it be. The whole 'representation' rests upon an illusion that means, an X is made for an U. But we want no more illusions; and then the Parliamentary stable forage is more expensive than pasturage upon the democratic parish common. Well, in the first place, we must elect, so let us choose people of intellect, heart, and independence!"

Hermann with his Bardolph nose, that constant light-house in his face, expressed his entire concurrence with the Doctor by a powerful shake of the hand, while Sengen, a very thoughtful man, who made a short pause between every word, and between every thought a pause of several bars, expressed his doubts still as to whether his tenants would be capable of entertaining any

97

opinion whatever about the welfare of the state.

In the meanwhile the Landrath had appeared a kindly old gentleman, a friend of Schönd and Auerswaldd, an enlightened, tolerant man, as far as the burning question was concerned, a supporter of the National Assembly, and much prepossessed in Blanden's favour, whose spirit he admired; he was the latter's most important ally. It is true he was not greatly beloved in the district; many landowners were displeased at the mildness of his rule, and also that at the Landrath's office, the superior court of corporal punishment, a mode of discipline used to bring up an improved race, was exercised in so inefficient a manner. With him came Baron von Fuchs, a perfect gentleman, who reminded one of the *roccoco* days, and distinguished himself by being utterly free from all prejudices. But he could not act with the same freedom, as he owned a wife of principles, a categorical imperative mood in petticoats.

Oberamtmann Werner of Schlohitten, entered the room noisily: he had first driven up to the sheepfold.

"You must sell me the new ram, Herr von Blanden; no refusal! I want it!"

"I do not sell my rams," replied Blanden.

"I will pay well, think it over! Besides, all respect for your sheepfold, my compliments to it! Not quite Schlohitten, upon my honour! The last touch so to say is wanting, the finer shades; but if I did not sit amidst the Schlohitten wool, I should gladly do so amidst that of Kulmitten!"

The reception room filled more and more, several elderly gentlemen with the iron cross upon their breasts appeared, at last also Herr Milbe, of Kuhlwangen, who again had not been in Kuhlwangen, but whom the note of invitation had found at the house of some intimate friend, where he had been engaged in a three days' game of *ombre*.

The uncomfortable mood which oppresses people's spirits before large dinners, as well as the craving of the inner man, by which the mind also is forced into an unwonted state of expectation, at first prevented all animated conversation, although the powerful organs of one or two agriculturists were thus able to assert themselves.

Dinner was served in the hall; the windows with their stained glass pictures did not allow the dazzling sunshine to penetrate, but shed a soft twilight, which so greatly enhances the enjoyments of a feast; the splendid table appointments, the bouquets of flowers in elegant vases, the tasteful arrangement of the table in the hall, which the slender pillar supported, and whose vaulted arch seemed to form the rays of a sun of stone, dispensed a sensation of comfort which unconsciously communicated itself to the guests.

The stone flags of the floor, too, awoke historical recollections, for the spurs of the brave knights of the Order once upon a time clattered over these stones.

The dinner took its course almost in accordance with the programme, which that cunning Wegen had drawn up in the wine cellar; gradually minds and spirits became more lively, the gentlemen with the iron cross told of Leipzig and Waterloo, the Oberamtmann of Schlohitten of his ewes, Baron von Fuchs of a few adventures of the East Prussian *haute volée*. The old Landrath led the general conversation to the absorbing topic; he spoke of Schön and Stein with that warmth which for all ages has distinguished the staunch friends of their Fatherland in East Prussia; he was only interrupted by Herr Milbe's noisy explanations, who sought to prove to his neighbour, that yesterday he must positively have won a *grand* at *ombre* if he had played *spadille* at once and called for *basta*.

"Our King," said the Landrath, "is an intellectual gentleman; he is even enthusiastic about the English state of affairs, about the land of inherited wisdom, and would be very comfortable with the Parliamentary system, because he himself is a man of great eloquence and knows how to value the results of clever speeches; but his unhappy affection for a romantic view of the State's system, in which he is strengthened by pietistic advisers, prevents him fulfilling former promises about the National Assembly; he fears to destroy the nimbus of the crown, and to endanger a divine right, which is confided to his faithful keeping."

"We are no backwoodsmen here," cried Milbe, "they shall learn that in Germany; here in East Prussia there are men who know what they want. The National Assembly is the *spadille* with which we will win the game."

"Our King has sense," interposed Baron von Fuchs, "he has ideas which Voltaire might envy him, although no greater contrast can be conceived than that which exists between the French scoffer's views of life and those of our King, so devoted to religious romance; but spell-bound as he is by a philosophy and poetry, which represent the charm of the moonlight-enchanted nights of the middle ages, as suitable ideas for the enlightened days of the present time, yet he has a perfect appreciation of new ideas, and his decisions can be so little counted upon, that I should not be amazed if he suddenly placed himself at the head of the political movement, and bore the banner in his own hand before us all."

"Until then," said Hermann, for whose political fervour his nose, already in a state of red-heat, was the best gauge, "we will trust to our own strength."

And, at the same time, he struck the table until the glass of Johannisberger before him fell over.

Doctor Kuhl cried enthusiastically—

"That is right! This trial of our own strength pleases me! Thus may all perish that comes from Metternich!"

"Only do not pour away the child with the bath," cried Baron Fuchs. "Johannisberger is a delicious wine, even although the dove of Patmos does not fly around Johannisberg, and his revelations have always become fatal to the German people—pale messengers of death, like the riders in the Apocalypse!"

"If we talk of biblical wines," cried Kuhl, "then I prefer the '*Lachrimæ Christi*.' It grows on fire-belching Vesuvius, and the future of nations only flourishes upon the volcanic ground of revolution."

"Heaven preserve us from revolutions!" cried the Landrath.

"As regards Johannisberger," said Fuchs, as he drank off his glass with gusto, "we will grant ample acknowledgment to our host's exquisite wine. But Prince Metternich may remind us of Goethe's verse—

'Ein echter deutscher Mann mag keinen Franzmann
leiden
Doch seine Weine trinkt er gern!'"

"Drink, gentlemen, drink!" Wegen continually repeated his invitation, as he hastened from chair to chair. "Best of Barons, of what use are your beautiful speeches—your glass is empty! Herr Milbe of Kuhlwangen, *tournez, tournez,* Johannisberger is trump! Dear Doctor Kuhl do not think of '*Lachrimæ Christi*' and the people's tears; taste this glorious flower of the reaction!"

Wegen did not need to urge Oberamtmann Werner, he had already done good work, and his neighbour, Sengen, listened, with sleepy resignation to the hymns in praise of sheep-breeding, which the best wool-producer in East Prussia sang in a voice becoming more and more maudlin.

"Two things we must have here—a National Assembly and better wool. A National Diet and wool market—those are the two vital arteries in political as in agricultural life. There is no truly free people without wool! The fine kinds, that is the principal matter. In what are we in advance of the Australians? We have no kangaroos, but we have no superfine sheep either. And in Silesia; do you see, Silesia is bestirring itself also; the States are bestirring themselves; there is intelligence in the province. The Breslau wool market proves that. I am a good patriot, yes I am," continued he, in a voice stifled with tears, "but if a man will be useful to his Fatherland, it does not merely depend upon how he votes, it does not merely depend upon the speeches that are made, it also depends upon the wool that is shorn. You understand me, Sengen, oh, we understand one another, brotherly heart!"

Sengen could only make his assent known by an animated shake of the head; for he, too, was so moved that his halting speech had become one great pause.

"The National Assembly would have a much better chance," said Hermann, in a loud, ringing voice, "if the Königsberg Jews did not also desire to have them."

"But, dear Hermann," said Kuhl, appeasingly, "the Promised Land they will never obtain, so that surely they must desire something else for themselves."

By the time that the champagne arrived, the general state of mind had attained that height which is usually succeeded by social chaos. It was, indeed, time for Blanden, who, until now, had taken little part in the conversation, to come forward with the political purpose that he associated with this dinner.

He rose, and immediately silence ensued—a compliment not only considered his due as host, but also on account of his personal position.

"While offering a welcome to all my guests," he began, "at the same time I take this opportunity to convey to you a wish which fills me at this present moment. In a short time, the election for the vacancy, which it has become necessary to fill up in our Provincial Diet, will take place, and I now introduce myself as a candidate to you, my guests, the most respected representatives of the district."

"Bravo! bravo!" cried the Landrath, and several gentlemen applauded also, while others, as Wegen remarked, became uneasy, and crumpled their dinner napkins under the table.

"Candid speech must be permitted; I will beg for no vote that is not given to me from free conviction; yet I know that I stand upon the same ground as all my guests. A new political epoch has dawned for Prussia; our Provincial Diets can no longer have any other aim than that of giving place to one general Prussian Diet, and this will one day be dismissed for a free constitution. Prussia must become a Constitutional State, like the advanced ones of the West; that is its vocation. It languishes beneath the contradictory fact that its internal arrangements, its organisations of defence, the regulations of its towns and districts are animated by a Liberal spirit, while the building lacks the necessary consummation. That which Stein, Schön, and Scharnhorst have begun tends to this consummation; it was the signal for supreme promises, and yet the coronation of the building has been left unfinished to the present day. The Bureaucratic Guard-room is to compensate to us for the Chamber of Parliament. The Prussian State is a *torso*; the educated circles of the people have become aware of it. Like a fresh breath, full of a future, it percolates through the whole nation; who could shut himself up from this vivifying breath? To become security for these recognised rights with power and determination, is the task which I have set to myself, and which I would further in the place where that word has gained a significant power for the State. Through the Provincial Diet to the National Diet is my watchword. Continued furtherance of Stein's and Scharnhorst's arrangements in the advanced spirit of the time! Then Prussia, which, until now, was only a doubtful Great Power, will occupy a position befitting it, and cast its old sword of Brennus, the sword of Frederick the Great, of Blücher and Gneisenau once more into the scale of European destinies. Released from the political followers opposed to the Austrian Chancellor of the State, it will again become the kingdom of Frederick the Great, that rests upon its own strength."

"We are all unanimous thereupon," cried Werner von Schlohitten, and a general jubilant applause proved this unanimity.

"Her von Blanden, he is our man," rang Hermann's deep bass.

"But you will permit us one question?" cried Milbe. "Questions are permitted not only in *ombre*, and candidates for election may be examined."

"That is my great desire," replied Blanden.

"You are in favour of a National Assembly," continued Milbe; "that is good! A National Assembly is *spadille*, but there is still a *basta*, a second trump which we wish to play out in East Prussia. Thunder and lightning! we here are in favour of healthy human understanding, and there in Berlin they want to pull the night-cap over our ears again. We believe in our good Lord, but we are told to believe in all possible miracles. Thus we should come to a nice state of *codille* with our politics. False piety has become the fashion; our foals are already ordered to graze in these melancholy meadows. *Sapperment* —we need men who do not love to grope about in such darkness; men like old Dinter, who went about in schools shedding the light of enlightenment. If all the world sits like a dummy, the game of *ombre* would cease. But we in Prussia still have the best games in our hand, and will not, for a longtime yet, write the world's history in a kettle; we will not be nor remain dark men."

"That we will not, that we will not!" cried all, unanimously.

"Truly not," added Blanden, with sharp emphasis.

"Well, then, Herr von Blanden," said Milbe, with great intrepidity, and the same demeanour with which he announced a dangerous game at *ombre*, "that is just the point. That is the evil of it!"

Baron von Fuchs pulled Milbe's coat-tail, the Landrath raised his fore-finger warningly, Wegen signed to him to stop, as he was accustomed to sign to the sentinels to cease when the latter saluted him in his lieutenant's uniform. But Milbe would not allow himself to be over-ruled.

"They say of you, Herr von Blanden, that you belong to the pious people, and, indeed, to that pious people who conducted themselves strangely in Königsberg. Thunder and lightning! it was out of the frying-pan into the fire. For anything I care, each may worship what he likes, and there have been plenty of strange saints in the world. If one man in his private chapel worships a stark-naked goddess of simply foaming meerschaum, I have nothing against it! but I should fight against it tooth and nail if such like were to become universal. I will not give my vote to the man who defends it, because he is not to my taste in religion, and similarity of taste, after all, is the principal thing, even in sacred matters."

Death-like stillness reigned around the table. Milbe's probe had touched the most vulnerable spot.

"In smoky Albertina, on the Pregel, we had a clever man, named Kant. I have read nothing of his, but I know he loved pure reason—and that, too, is my feeling; with pure want of reason I will have nothing to do. And that nourished in Königsberg," added Milbe, as he struck the table with his hand, "and it is infectious as small-pox, and our deputies shall issue an order for quarantine against it. I demand that, as truly as I am Milbe, of Kuhlwangen, and seldom in Kuhlwangen."

"It is ten years," replied Blanden, in a firm, calm voice, "since I went astray amidst those sects whose conduct I myself must now repudiate. The charm of something strange and uncommon prompted me; I was an enthusiast. Yet even in those days already I found a shoal where I had sought a haven. That lies far behind me; I have set oceans and hemispheres between myself and my past. Man errs so long as he strives. But in me every trace of enthusiasm is extinguished; my thoughts are no longer fixed upon what is mystery, will no longer seek that boundary line where the ocean, with its dark abyss, touches the sky with its bright planets. Least of all do I lean to that piety which is favoured for State reasons, and that infects the fresh life of the present with the sickly shadow of a romance long since buried. T reject the barriers of faith and conscience that are painted in the colours of the State. That which we then sought erringly was at least our own free action, an outflow of inward light; we put our whole soul into the sect of the Free Elect. It was a community of men of the same mind who were even looked askant upon by the Government. But as I am now, I stand firmly and entirely upon the ground of a Free-thinker; no sentimental extravagance has any more power over me. What Kant and his successors struggled for has become the atmosphere of my mental life, and I am ready for the most resolute defiance, like you all, if a relapse into misty credulity or fettered Government hypocrisy would destroy that which the labour of great thinkers has built up in more than half a century."

"Hem, there is something in that," said Milbe, with vigorous eulogy.

"Long live reason," cried Wegen, and the glasses were clinked merrily. Oberamtmann Werner, too, shook Blanden heartily by the hand, as he was already in a much affected mood.

"Yes, yes, these false saints are the wolves in sheep's clothing, as it says in the Bible. A good breeder of sheep must entertain especial horror of them. And I have it, I have it! Yes, brotherly heart, if you abjure it, that lamb-like pious sanctity of former days, that kissing, love-making and hypocrisy of the pious people—sweet as sugar, from the upper Haberberge—then you may still be worth something. You can represent the province capitally. You have my vote because your sheep are in good condition, and an agriculturist's intelligence is known by the fleece of his sheep. Clink glasses, brotherly heart! Only no future pious giddiness!"

The dinner company had already broken up into noisy groups. Once more the Landrath became spokesman, and by the esteem in which he was held, had been able to obtain silent hearers—

"Herr von Blanden has expressed all our sentiments; as worthy deputy from our province, he will fix his mind upon the whole. Our politics are patch-work until a general constitution forms a piece of mosaic into one organisation, and without Frederick the Great's free, tolerant spirit, our Prussia, under the hands of the *virorum obscurorum*, will never, never raise itself to a brilliant position. Let us return thanks to our host for having expressed an opinion which we all share, and let us empty our glasses to his health!"

The guests' favourable sentiments found this to be the most suitable mode of expression, and at the same time the election dinner came to a termination. Now good humour began to display itself undisturbedly. Some danced upon the stone flags of the old hall of the Order, while the evening sun was already flooding the dark stained glass windows with glowing fire. Baron von Fuchs stood in one corner of the room, and had assembled an extensive circle of listeners around him; for he poured out a large *cornucopiæ* of most interesting anecdotes which related to the nobility of the neighbouring district. There were seductions and abductions, tales of prodigality, legacy-hunting, insanity, and idiotcy; and the Baron understood how to relate all so fluently and adroitly, that the gentlemen listened with great enjoyment, as though these sad human traits existed for their amusement only. Milbe tried in vain to get a party for *ombre* together; even the Oberamtmann could not be roused. He already lay in a state of semi-somnolence in a cushioned chair, with blissfully transfigured features, and dreamed of golden fleeces. Doctor Kuhl, on the other hand, delighted the peasant squires with his athletic performances, by balancing the heaviest chairs upon his finger tips. Coffee was then drunk in the park, which was illuminated with lights and gay-coloured lanterns; Olkewicz had arranged everything in the best possible manner. Anyone going to the pond could see Kuhl tread water.

It was late in the evening when the guests called for their carriages.

"The feast has fulfilled my greatest expectations," said Wegen to Blanden, when the last had departed.

"And yet," replied the latter, "it lies like a nightmare upon my mind. I must for ever gaze into the hated magic mirror which every one holds before me, in order to see my distorted reflection. And if they all seem, in brightest mood, to forget that which in their hearts they cherish against me, and which obstructs the path of my desires, only some chance is needed which would awaken the past more vividly, and they would all stand against me once more. Just as it is impossible to commence life again from the beginning, so is it also impossible entirely to shake off one's past. Herculean power is wanted to cast this burden from one; I often despair of it. Well, I shall, it is to be hoped, be more successful in love than in politics. I shall hasten to bring my beloved one home."

Despite Wegen's supremely cheerful state of mind and freedom from care, Blanden could not overcome his melancholy mood on that evening. Until long after midnight, he sat on the balcony above the lake, and gazed out over the monotonous surface, and the enigma of human life rested heavily upon his soul.

CHAPTER X.

THE PROPOSAL.

In Warnicken, the Regierungsrath was again engaged in eager dispute with the Kreisgerichtsrath; his disposition was an unfriendly one. Nothing was heard of Blanden, and ever again the thought arose in old Kalzow that he and his Miranda might have imperilled Eva's good name by their thoughtless encouragement. Even one single such sad, disagreeable thought suffices, especially when people are up in years, to cast a shadow over their whole life. It is not like a poisonous fungus that grows quietly in the shade; it is like a bursting dust-ball which, at the least touch, covers us from head to foot with its deadly contents.

Warnicken had suddenly become wearisome to the Regierungsrath; always the Wolfs-schlucht, and the Fuchs-spitze, and the monotonous sound of the breakers, and the usually bad dinner, and the Liberal Kreisgerichtsrath, who daily became more unbearable. At the same time the intolerable heat; everything was uncomfortable for him, even his flannel jacket, and his big white neck-cloth, and at times even his Miranda.

The latter, too, was not exactly in a roseate temper, and she exposed her majestic side more than usual, especially to those who stood nearest to her throne.

Political questions were now but little discussed with the Kreisgerichtsrath; as regards politics, the Regierungsrath was very reserved; but were there not a hundred other subjects about which they could hold opposite views, and the Regierungsrath now always was of an opposite opinion from every other mortal with whom he commenced a conversation.

It was a sultry summer evening, when Kalzow, with his wife and the Kreisgerichtsrath, sat on the Fuchs-spitze. The sun was inclining to its rest, and cast glowing lights into the waves. Yet it was still so hot that the Regierungsrath laid his straw hat beside him upon the bench, and continually made movements betokening such craving for freedom, as though he would jump out of his cravat, and occasionally even out of his skin.

"To-day there were eighty degrees of heat in the shade," said the Kreisgerichtsrath, as he wiped away the drops of perspiration.

"Thirty degrees, I say thirty degrees," retorted Kalzow, irritatedly.

"Eight-and-twenty degrees Réaumur," said the Kreisgerichtsrath, with quiet decision.

"Réaumur! Of course, Réaumur. What have we to do with Fahrenheit or Celsius?"

"The astronomists measure by Celsius."

"I am no star-gazer, and decline any such inuendoes," said Kalzow, while coughing annoyedly. "Unfortunately, people have enough to do to watch their own feet, so that they may not stumble upon earth."

Miranda sighed, while her knitting needles began to move nervously.

The Kreisgerichtsrath shrugged his shoulders, and drew figures in the sand; he knew well that for his friend he played the part that in sham-fights the appointed enemy does, against whom all manœuvres are directed. Yet he was not prepared for so vigorous an onslaught as that with which the Regierungsrath surprised him.

"Indeed, it is impossible to bear with you any longer," continued the latter. "You contradict one constantly; do you then, think that it makes intercourse pleasant in such heat? I have put a seal upon politics—I do not allude to that tender theme any more; can one give greater proofs of peaceable intentions? I am contented with everything, with general assemblies, even, for anything that I care, with the French revolution; I allow it all to be discharged over me like torrents of rain, and do not even put up an umbrella before it; but you seek quarrels, you do! Can there be anything more harmless than the lines in a thermometer to which the mercurial column extends its tongue; no, even for that the alarm-drum must be beaten. Quarrelling, everlasting quarrelling, here where one ought to recruit oneself; I can bear it no longer!"

A violent fit of coughing closed this bayonet charge upon his patient friend.

The Kreisgerichtsrath rose with great calmness and said—

"I can give no better proofs of my peaceable intentions than by retiring," and he disappeared upon the footpath that led to the valley.

This retreat did not much improve Kalzow's temper, for he felt it to be his own moral defeat. Much excited, he walked to and fro, and was not disinclined to make the only person who could still be called to account, responsible for all the evil which lay in the air to-day; yet, a glance at her, and the challenging manner in which she handled her knitting needles, proved sufficiently to him that this fort was fully armed and ensured against any surprise, and that in an attack upon it he should be running great danger.

Therefore, he sat down again beside his wife, after he had soothed his internal excitement by several pinches of snuff, and commenced a peaceful conversation.

"What has become of Eva?"

"The girl wanted to read something, and then water the flowers."

"How do you think she is?"

"As usual—quiet, and sometimes in a happier state of mind than formerly."

"She has perfect confidence?"

"So far, she has not uttered a word of doubt."

"Well, then, all will be right! She has Blanden's promise, and I take him to be a man of his word."

"Certainly, at least, we will hope it, although it is a sad experience that even the best of men, whose word at other times is firm as a rock, always waver in love. That is an abandoned territory; there begins the great comedy of life, behind the scenes of which one can never see properly."

"Come, it is hardly so bad."

"Nor married men, dear Kalzow, do I trust entirely; they are the worst kind; but we will draw a veil over that—it is best to do so!"

"But if Blanden even keep his word, supposing, indeed, that he has given it, about which the contract is not yet signed—you know my sister has, it is true, consented that we should adopt her daughter, because, to a certain extent, public opinion demanded it; yet she attached the condition thereto, that her daughter's betrothal should immediately be announced to her, and she be invited to any celebration of it; under any circumstances, she will make the bridegroom's acquaintance as soon as possible."

"We cannot prevent that, dear Kalzow; and, after all, what she requires is reasonable. On such an occasion the unnatural barrier should fall that separates her from her daughter. Certainly, this sister-in-law is like an evil spirit to me; she spoils our social reputation; we have always kept her aloof from her daughter, and only sent her regular reports as to the latter's well-being; Eva herself has never been allowed to write to her; such a total separation was unavoidable."

"But what will Blanden say to that mother?"

"From what one hears, neither had anything wherewith to reproach themselves; he probably knows them; they moved in the same circles for some time."

"That is quite possible! All the same, it will be hard for me to point her out as the girl's mother; nor is it in truth, necessary, she has no longer any right over the girl. Should she, however, come to the betrothal, nothing will remain for us but to raise the veil. But where is Eva? The worst would be if we troubled our heads about matters which, indeed, exist nowhere but in our brains; day after day passes, and Blanden does not return."

While the married couple thus exchanged their anxieties and fears, their looks were suddenly arrested by a boat gliding over the sea.

The Regierungsrath had a perfect right to cough, because his telescope did not deceive him; it was Eva who, instead of reading and watering the flowers in the garden, let herself once again be rocked upon the ocean's waves, with the idiot fisherman's girl.

"A disobedient child," said the Regierungsräthin, annoyed; "there is something erratic about her; she does not belie her mother's blood."

"Yet her father, who died early, was an honourable man; he only committed the fault of trying to use a will-o'-the-wisp as a night-light."

"Fie, Kalzow."

"She is my sister, and yet she was not worthy of so good a man as the captain; from her youth upwards she was a strange creature, enthusiastically dreamy, often wild and eager for pleasure. Eva, fortunately, takes more after her father than her mother."

Meanwhile Eva had landed and wandered, singing, up the Fuchs-spitze.

"Naughty girl! You wanted to be taken captive again," her foster-father cried to her, his good humour having gradually been restored during his conversation with Miranda.

"Oh, no, papa! I am already a captive," said Eva, smiling.

"Disobedience merits punishment," interposed her stern mother! "we will leave you at home on our next pleasure party."

"Then Salomon will be thoroughly miserable," retorted Eva, laughing.

"And Herr von Blanden does not come," said the Rath, assuming the air of a judge of assizes. "You both have a little conspiracy between you; but he promised to return soon."

"Do not be uneasy, papa! He has more important business at home than here, but as he pledged his word he is sure to come."

"I suppose the mermaids sang that to you?"

"What do mermaids know of a man's word? But I know that it is firm and unchanging, and that one may sleep quietly beneath its care, as if under angels' wings."

She said this in an elevated voice, and a transfiguring radiancy seemed to pass over her features. Her parents also soon felt calmed by Eva's indomitable trust. The Rath would gladly have directed a few more questions to the girl, but Salomon's arrival interrupted the conversation.

The latter came breathlessly up the hill.

"I know something, Fräulein Eva, but even I can keep my secrets to myself."

"Then you—"

"Redeem it, as one does in playing at forfeits!"

"I am not inclined to play."

"I believe it! The sun is setting so beautifully, it makes one think—

'The maid stood by the ocean,

And long and deep sighed she,

With heartfelt sad emotion

The setting sun to see.'"[1]

"But, my dear Salomon," said Eva, "we know our Heine by heart."

"'Sweet maiden, why this fretting?
An olden trick is here,'"

Salomon continued to recite unabashedly, and then added—

"Heine pleases me actually better than Schiller; one feels more at ease with him. Everything about Schiller is more solemn, one must appear in full dress, and be led about in nothing but state apartments, where one feels shy of sitting down. With Heine, one enters a cosy drinking party; all sit down in shirt sleeves, and one hastens to pull off one's own coat."

"That would be like playing nine-pins," said Eva.

"Certainly, the poet always meets the Nine; he scoffs at false sentiment, and in life, as in society, there is so much false sentiment; it is just as in the Palais Royal in Paris, where I went last holidays with mamma. The shops with sham diamonds and precious stones are to be found side by side with those full of genuine jewellery, and, at the first glance, one cannot distinguish the imitation. Therefore, our thanks are due to the man who has taught us the true and the false by his scoffing remarks. Even with Schiller, false jewels of sentiment are to be found. Laura at the piano! excuse me. I have seen many a girl sit at the piano, who did not play badly either, but never have I thought when doing so of 'Cocytus' waves of tears,' or of 'the suns which arise from out the giant arms of chaos,' or even the verse, 'Lips, cheeks, burned and quivered.' That is not the way people kiss! I have never noticed anything of the sort. Or even Thecla, who looks upon her lover as a good angel, who would carry her pick-a-back up the mountains! What a picture of bad taste! And we are to rave about that? Fräulein, will you know my secret now?"

"Not yet, Herr Salomon."

"Then, you see, a great deal of poetical rubbish is talked about these sunsets. After all, it is quite natural, and it is connected with the earth's revolution that the sun seems to set, and its rays break into gay colours through the denser strata of vapour on the horizon. But it is really childish to go into ecstasies about those few bright colours; it is the same pleasure that the soap-bubbles inspire in childish minds; and yet such things are sung in all metres of verse. And there is also an ode, which we had to learn by rote, and begins with the lines—

'Sun, thou sinkest,
Sun, thou sinkest,
Sink in peace then, oh, thou sun!'

It is, I believe, by a certain Kosegarten, who bore a very well-known and much promising name, but, alas! was a parson, somewhere near some large waters, whence he drew his poetry. Then comes Heine, and calls the sunset an 'old piece;' capital, and how the scales fall from our eyes. That is the man for me! Do not you rave about 'Lorelei,' too, my Fräulein? Should you not like to be a 'Lorelei?'"

"Papa would first have to buy me a golden comb."

"And what will you give for my secret?"

"Still nothing, Herr Salomon."

"Well, I am disinterested, my Fräulein!

'My blossoming life thou hast poisoned,
And made it hateful to me.'

But I revenge myself nobly! I know that my communication will cause you pleasure; and, besides, I know that I shall be grieved at your pleasure; I know that I cannot reckon upon the least reward as messenger—and yet—I will make the communication—Herr von Blanden has just arrived."

The effect of the news was, indeed, greater than even Salomon had expected. Rath and Räthin started up from the bench, with countenances radiant with pleasure! Eva stood as if transfigured with blissful delight in the last gleam of the evening's glow, and folded her hands.

Yes, she even vouchsafed a kindly smile and a word of thanks to the head scholar. The latter had greeted Herr von Blanden immediately upon his arrival, as he drove up to the inn, and informed him where he should find the Kalzow family. Therefore, it was decided to await him up here. Eva's heart beat violently; she did not listen to her parents' remarks, which suddenly spent themselves in Blanden's praise, his punctuality and reliability, still less to Salomon's recitals, which scattered abundant daring allusions and poetical quotations, in order to console himself for the fresh triumphs which his rival celebrated.

"Did I not say that I should give you pleasure?

'To all, its arms doth Mirth unfold,
And every heart forgets its cares—
And Hope is busy in the old.'

But I bear a striking resemblance to Cassandra, and wander like her—

'Unjoyous in the joyful throng.'

It is so charming to be so watched for, greeted with such delight! This Blanden! But one must console oneself—

'With careless hands they mete our doom,
Our woe or welfare, Hazard gives
Patroclus slumbers in the tomb.'

And still it is melancholy—

'Gleams my love in beauty's splendour,

Like the child of ocean's foam,

As his bride my mistress tender

Is a stranger taking home.'"

Eva would have been best pleased to hasten down the footpath to meet her beloved one, if she had been free to follow her heart's impulses.

Blanden came at last, and she only greeted him with a cordial shake of the hand. The scholar averted his gaze, and looked at the sea that was already playing in the ashen grey tints of dusk; no more verses arose to his mind. The

Rath was full of amiability.

"We expected you in vain both yesterday and the previous day; however, the harvest, the harvest! I know what importance that is on large estates; the well-filled barns, the ricks in all the fields; because it is a bountiful year. In Kulmitten you cultivate more wheat; I know that, and in Nehren the soil is more adapted for rye."

"And you are sure to part reluctantly from your castle," added the Räthin. "No doubt you have a fine orangery, splendid flower beds! That is wanting here. Nature here is somewhat wild! I like order. Hedges of yew—I am passionately fond of them! Have you yew in your park?"

"Everything that you wish, *gnädige* Frau, every kind of indigenous and exotic weeds! But the most beautiful flower I have still to transplant to my park. Herr Rath, Frau Räthin, may I beg you to grant me a serious conversation at your house?"

"We are at your service, at your service," said the Rath, as he seized his hat quickly, pushed his chin back expectantly into his neck-cloth, and in all his movements evinced eager promptitude. Miranda was also ready for a speedy departure, like a proud frigate that is about to raise its anchor.

Eva stood, her hand pressed upon her heart, and, with Salomon, slowly followed them as they hastened away.

It was rather tranquillising for her when the former deemed this moment to be a favourable one in which to make a declaration of love to her, which she declined with kind decision; it relieved the moment's state of tension.

Salomon, having received this rebuff, did not think he ought to linger longer in Eva's vicinity. He bade her a cold farewell and sped back to the Fuchs-spitze.

Below, in the modest reception-room, in which the smoky beams were pasted over with the cheapest sheets of pictures of Neu-Ruppin, Blanden spoke the decisive word. He proposed for Eva's hand, he promised to make her happy, he explained that his circumstances permitted him to relinquish any dowry, that he did not need to enquire as to her fortune, that in herself he found the greatest treasure, the greatest riches with which he would now adorn his life.

Bright tears of joy glistened in the old Rath's eyes, and Miranda also wept. It was a strange scene; who had ever seen the Regierungsräthin Kalzow, that stony Niobe, weep? But both loved Eva with all their hearts, even although in their own way, and now to be able to greet her as a rich, aristocratic mistress of a castle, was indeed delightful.

After having given his consent, the Rath said, hesitatingly, "I am too happy to be able to welcome you as my future son-in-law; although only my consent is needed, yet I must inform you that we are merely the girl's adopted parents. Her father is dead, her mother still lives upon a small estate that her husband, a captain, left to her; she is my sister; she will not fail to be present at her daughter's wedding or betrothal."

"She will be welcome to us," said Blanden; "I repeat, that it does not trouble me whether, from you or her real mother, Eva has any prospects of inheritance. Are not all my possessions hers, so soon as the union is sealed, and now I pray you summon Eva, and give us your blessing."

Evidently Eva's family was wearisome to Blanden; all information about them was void of interest for him, he hoped so soon as possible to deliver her from this irksome connection. Her mother was Kalzow's sister. He was not very eager to make her acquaintance. The dreary atmosphere of this narrow-minded, prosaic life, should no longer oppress his Eva, and even the thought of two mothers-in-law did not disturb him farther; he had confidence in his power to hold as much aloof from the one as from the other.

Eva appeared: she was full of joy and happiness—was it not only what she had expected? Mother Miranda gazed with certain pride upon her child; she began already to treat the future aristocratic lady with certain consideration, and to clothe her faultfinding in a pleasant garb. She suddenly looked upon Eva with totally different eyes; she had formerly never thought that she should feel any respect for this little girl.

Blanden folded Eva closely and impetuously to his heart, he said silently to himself: "Now I begin a new life; now I place a boundary and sign-stone to my past; the future of my whole life depends upon this moment! May it smile as kindly upon me as do the wonderful eyes of this glorious girl!" But then he said in joyful excitement—"As I would proclaim my happiness to the world, so do I feel the need for others to rejoice with me! We will celebrate our betrothal in the largest, most extensive circle; let that be my care, Herr Rath! To arrange the solemnization of the marriage according to the country's custom, be yours; in that I will not interfere with you, but the betrothal celebration confide to me."

"But it will be difficult for you, here in Warnicken," began the Räthin.

"It is impossible here," interrupted Blanden. "I must beg you all to migrate to Neukuhren for a few days. It possesses a Kursaal, and merry company; many of my friends are there. I will make arrangements for an entertainment in that place, and all Kuhren shall be invited."

"Shall we not rather enjoy our happiness alone?" asked Eva, pressing closely to her lover.

"I am proud of you, and will show all the world that I am so; you must let me have my own way in this matter."

The entertainment at Neukuhren flattered her parent's pride; they gave their consent, and undertook to take lodgings there a few days later, so as to assist in his preparations. Of course, Blanden said, all the visitors staying at Warnicken were included in the invitation; neither the Kriesgerichtsrath nor Salomon, nor Minna with her envious mother were to be omitted.

The particular evening was decided upon, everything planned. Miranda possessed courage sufficient not to dread the troubles of a migration, and never had Rath Kalzow's pipe seemed so enjoyable to him as on that evening.

But Blanden wished to enjoy the sanctity of those hours alone with Eva; they granted themselves leave of absence, and walked towards the sea. The idiot ocean-maiden lay on the sand beside her boat, and stared fixedly at the east, where the moon was just rising deeply red out of the waters; she did not look unlike a seal.

"Käthe, we wish to row on the sea," Blanden called to her. Quickly as lightning the girl arose, kissed his hand, sprang into the boat and seized the oar.

Soon the lovers were rocking upon the slightly disturbed waters.

Käthe kept good time with her oars, but glared as if amazed when Blanden and Eva exchanged kisses and embraces. On the first occasion she even let the oars drop while she folded her hands.

The moon meanwhile had risen entirely, and silvered the wide expanse of the East Sea, the bare cliffs, the green ravines, but a cold wind swept from the north. The waves rose higher, the boat began to roll. Blanden pressed his beloved one firmly to himself, to protect her from the raw north wind; she looked into his eyes, and so avoided the sight of the rolling gunwales, and at the same time the discomfort of dizziness.

Above brightly sparkled the Polar star, Cassiopea, the Milky-way; but it seemed as though, by the boat's uncertain motion, even the heavenly stars began to rock.

It was a disagreeable voyage. Eva shivered; Blanden could not help thinking of the excursions in boats on Lago Maggiore, of the warm breath that glided over the magic lake, of the enchanting delight of a southern night; but the young life that was pressed so trustingly to his side had given itself up for ever to him; how differently his heart was stirred by it from what it was by that mysterious beauty who only broke one or two jewels out of her crown for him.

"This is yours, confided to your protection for a whole life-time!" With that thought he replied to the questions which seemed to be directed to his heart from Eva's widely-opened, gazelle-like eyes.

Louder became the roaring of the distant waves; Käthe, without waiting for orders, guided the boat back to the shore. And the billows, rearing themselves up ever higher, came rolling on like serpents behind the young betrothed couple, tossing the skiff up and down. Eva's blooming features and cheeks paled, dizziness and discomfort took possession of her; it was time that the boat should reach the shore. Blanden was obliged to exert all his strength in assisting Käthe to land.

"The storm has put our young love to the test," said Blanden, "but we hold to one another in trouble and in joy, and defy danger."

Which Eva confirmed with a heartfelt kiss and fervent embrace.

The ocean-maiden, however, again lay upon the strand; the tempest raged above her; her red shawl fluttered in the wind; the waves must wet her feet.

Of what was she thinking?

Idiot Käthe loved Blanden and hated her rival.

CHAPTER XI.

IN NEUKUHREN.

During all these occurrences, life in the bathing-place, Neukuhren, continued on its course, like a wound-up watch. Professor Baute and Dr. Reising still lived upon a philosophical war-footing; Baute often maintained, with an energy which seemed to disarm any contradiction, that Hegel's philosophy was quite incomprehensible to any reasonable creature, that the somersaults of his ideas were only harlequinades of thought, and that if he had read a few chapters of logic he felt like the scholar of Faust—

"My brain with all that nonsense reels,
As if in my head revolved mill wheels."

Dr. Reising paled with internal annoyance, and bit his lips; he pushed his rebellious hair back from his head with a nervously trembling hand, but he took tall Albertina for an example, who, like a goddess of silence, always seemed to lay a finger upon his lips. He, too, was silent, and he had his reasons for it, he was now making great progress in the conquest of the Professor's seven daughters. Dr. Kuhl had advised him to fix his eyes upon one of two youngest, who had the longest future before them, and of whom, perhaps, something might still be made; but when, obediently to such experienced counsel, he devoted particular attention to Gretchen and Marie, he encountered a decided repulse, as the two foolish creatures did not know how to appreciate the great importance of a Hegelite. Gretchen and Marie, who quarrelled the live-long day, were only unanimous on one point—that Dr. Reising's nose had an ugly termination, and that there was something intolerably knowing in his mode of placing his finger upon it. Gretchen considered that his voice was too thin, that his words could be passed through the eye of a needle, and Marie said the Doctor appeared to her like a nibbling mouse.

Of what assistance was all Dr. Kuhl's wisdom? It was rendered futile by circumstances. Forced to retreat by the young troops, Reising met with better success before the old guards. He did not know himself how it came about, but Euphrasia, with her two Slavonian plaits, and her coquettish smile, had conquered his heart, and here, too, he encountered a readiness that was only ill concealed beneath mock-modest resistance. And she was the eldest.

To a head accustomed to think correctly, this was a decided advantage, for how much evil has not befallen many a family by the marriage of a younger daughter preceding that of an elder one. Surely everything in the world must be done in proper rotation. "In proper rotation" is one of the principles of creation, and the Doctor did little to offend them when he wooed the ripest beauty of the Baute family. But, from want of other conquests, as Dr. Kuhl was absent, and, according to report, was unattainable for several reasons, Ophelia and Lori had also resolved to be pleased with Reising, and to cast out their nets over him. Thus the Baute family performed a sort of "Midsummer Night's Dream," a rushing to and fro, seeking and evading ensued, such as only the sap of the wonderful flower, "Love-in-Idleness," can produce.

There they sat together in a jasmine bower, Reising and Euphrasia; he had caught her, and she had let herself be caught with pleasure. She sat there reading Puschkin's poems, and her two blonde plaits moved about most gracefully when she shook her head over any of the poet's bold or inadmissible thoughts.

He had come to her; at first she started at this surprise, but then resigned herself to the inevitable. As is befitting womanly modesty, when alone with a strange man, she did not venture to look straightly at him; now and again she cast a glance towards him, in which flashed as much meaning as possible.

"Puschkin is a great poet," said she, in a kind of ecstasy. "Indeed, I love the Russian poets; they are not such Philistines as the Germans. What views! One sees that they belong to a nation that rules the earth!"

"Very beautiful, Fräulein Euphrasia! But still the world is ruled by the mind, and it is the German mind that is called to the world's dominion."

"Herbart, or Hegel?" asked Euphrasia, smiling coquettishly.

"Oh, my Fräulein! You touch a very tender spot in my life; it makes me so sad that I cannot hold the same opinions as your father."

"Why sad?" asked Euphrasia. "Learned men are seldom of the same opinion."

"Oh, you know; you must know why it makes me sad!"

"Not at all," replied the fair one, smiling unconsciously.

"I should wish above everything that all men of intellect should recognise Hegel as their mental guide; what is more adapted to such guidance than a system which inculcates the progress of man in the consciousness of freedom. What does Herbart teach?—all respect to your father! Nothing of the sort! He confuses the good and the beautiful in a lamentable manner; nowhere does he speak of the progress of mankind. With him the mind is a *tabula rasa*, where different ideas agree to meet. Some are stronger, others weaker; they create a king of the rats, and hang one upon another. It is an excellent comedy; there some tumble down again headlong over the threshold of knowledge! Ah, my Fräulein! that may perhaps suit the ideas which one entertains when knitting stockings, but not the ideas which shall found the world's existence."

"Papa may be mistaken," said Euphrasia. "Our mother always maintained that he was mistaken, and if this occurred in matters that we understand, it is probably also the case in those that we do not comprehend."

"Schiller certainly maintained," continued Reising, "that only 'error is life, and knowledge is death,' but which German University could choose such a motto? Why, in that case all would be changed into churchyards, because knowledge is their life, and inconceivably much is known, my Fräulein!"

"Certainly, certainly, Herr Doctor, inconceivably much, and even by single individuals, yourself for instance," said Euphrasia, as she bowed humbly before Hegel's all-knowing pupil.

"At least a *horror vacui* assails us true disciples of knowledge from a Socratian standpoint. We are to know that we can know nothing; of what use, then, would be the search of a whole life-time? But, my Fräulein, it is not about that I would now speak with you. Even the difference of opinions is as old as the world, but I only wished to tell you that it is a misfortune if we, your father and I, cannot agree."

"Oh, there are some points," said Euphrasia, rather hastily, "about which this unanimity is not so difficult."

"Do you think so, my Fräulein?" said the Doctor, quickly, as he passed his hand several times through his bristly hair. "Oh, you make me happy—if I dared hope, yes, I must confess to you, I must—"

Just at this moment, when Euphrasia hung so devoutly upon the lips of the future private tutor that her plaits even forgot their otherwise wonted pendulum-like motions, malicious chance brought her two dear sisters, Ophelia and Lori, upon the scene, who, behind the creepers around the arbour, had listened, unperceived, to Reising's last outpourings, and now believed that the time had arrived for them to come forward.

"We bring interesting news, dear sister," said Lori, who spitefully remarked the effect produced by her appearance.

Euphrasia rose, glowing with anger, for such an interruption in one of the most beautiful moments of her life, and which promised to be still much more beautiful, had enraged her intensely. Doctor Reising, it is true, as Hegel's pupil, always looked upon chance as unreasoning, but this one appeared to be a stronger argument than ever in favour of the immortal master's doctrine than all other chances which had already befallen him in his young life.

"What is the matter?" asked Euphrasia, sternly. Her whole demeanour assumed an air of command, and had Reising been a better psychologist, he would have discovered no favourable reading of the horoscope for his wedded future in the tone and manner of his Euphrasia.

"We walked quickly," said Ophelia, "and wanted to rest for a moment."

And she sat down upon the bench, breathing with difficulty and sighing, and darted one of those glances, soft as velvet, which flatter a susceptible heart wonderfully, at Doctor Reising, who stood near her. Her eyes were furnished with long silken lashes, and as they were her sole recognised beauty, she had brought the skilful management of them to a most artistic state of perfection; she laid claim to sentimentality, which was peculiarly favoured by this dowry of Nature. When she cast her eyes modestly down, they disappeared almost entirely beneath their silken curtain; if she turned them up, it lay like a canopy above their rapturous glance. But Doctor Reising did not possess his friend Doctor Kuhl's versatility in the remotest degree. Ophelia's eyelashes had no power over him after Euphrasia's plaits had bound him in their fetters, and he looked coldly down upon those speaking, upturned eyes like a dreary, rainy sky upon two widely opened flower calyx.

"There is to be a large entertainment," said Lori, dancing to and fro. "Doctor Kuhl has just told us of it, and we came, dear sister, to bring you the glad news."

"What do I care about your entertainment?"

"Oh, we are all to be invited. Herr von Blanden has engaged himself in Warnicken, and to-morrow will celebrate his betrothal. They are to dance under the big pear tree."

The news was not without its effect upon Euphrasia; she leaned her head upon her hand, and said, thoughtfully—

"What shall we wear?"

"Our summer dresses, of course," replied Lori. "I, my sap-green, you, your violet. Ophelia, to be sure, has an ugly pink dress. The bodice is much too high; it makes her look like a *picotte*, with a stem that is broken near the top. Emma is sensible, and always wears dark clothes, but Albertina's white dress still bears traces of the last picnic, and is covered with every variety of soil. What our two little ones wear does not matter; no one notices those half-grown up creatures."

After this weighty affair had been quickly settled by loquacious Lori, Euphrasia found time to enquire who the bride was.

"A little girl from Warnicken," said Lori, in a tone of indifference. "The daughter of a Regierungsrath. She has no fortune, and opinions differ as to her beauty."

"Oh, heavens, what luck!" sighed Ophelia, "such a wealthy, noble landowner."

"Some say," continued Lori, "he had met her at the seaside in a wood, where she was standing, wreathed in garlands of leaves, like a dryad just stepped forth out of the trunk of an oak, and there she bewitched him, as nothing of the sort ever appeared to him in his own forests in Masuren. Others, on the contrary, say he met her on the sea; it was a novel kind of fishing, he himself was more the fish than the fisherman, as she has cast her net with great skill. Who can tell how it occurred? Besides, it is perfectly immaterial; the principal thing is, that to-morrow evening there will be dancing under the pear tree."

"But we must return," said Ophelia.

"We only came to fetch you. Herr von Blanden is going from table to table inviting the people; we must not delay. Doctor Kuhl will introduce us to him."

"Come, Doctor Reising!"

"There is no such great hurry," said Euphrasia. "I have seen Her von Blanden several times already, he does not interest me! I do not like those aristocratic landowners; certainly he looks very different from the rest; he has a pair of remarkable eyes, but in reality they are all moulded in the same fashion. So if you like, we will remain here."

But the sisterly rivals would not allow that, their eloquence on the subject was of such convincing power, or rather was so clad with thorns of every description, that the Doctor and the heiress of the house of Baute, found it most advisable to yield.

The visitors at Neukuhren were in a state of great excitement, the committee of amusement had announced its sittings to be permanent; all were invited by Blanden; all wished to prove their gratitude at the betrothal by some act or attention. A concert should precede the dance under the large pear tree; there was so much young musical talent, that a large amateur orchestra was easily formed, and all private performers had brought their instruments with them, so that any one strolling along the village street of Neukuhren on a quiet summer's evening would hear, now on the right, now on the left, sounds like wonderful solos of a separated band of musicians, to which chance often lent discordant symphony. An assessor who played first upon the cornet, then the trumpet, made himself most audible; people pretended to remark that the sea then always became particularly disturbed, as though the Tritons and Nereides stormed upon the strand because they were jealous of the competition with their shell-horns. One first and one second violin, who lived in two stories of the same house, sought to arrange an impossible harmony between the "Carnival of Venice" and the second's part in a quartett by Beethoven. The flute was played every evening by one of the stoutest proprietors in the district of Labian, who blew everything that he possessed into the holes of that oldest of wooden instruments. The smallest doctor who practised which the town of pure reason could produce, played the violoncello; he found numerous patients amongst his listeners, and had to be sought for behind his instrument where he was in danger of disappearing. A lawyer, white as dough, who on account of lack of legal knowledge wished to devote himself to a diplomatic career, also played the violoncello, and indeed so well that a brilliant future was prophecied for him as such artistic performances in drawing-rooms fit people for higher diplomatic posts. A great kettle-drum was also present in Neukuhren, but in this instance it belonged to a professional not an amateur: that might be the reason why, although it had been seen to be unloaded from the carriage, its existence remained a myth, and the artist seemed to content himself with one important part of his performance, with counting the pauses in the time.

The formation of the orchestra was entrusted to an unknown composer, who, it was said, had the manuscript of four operas lying in his work-room. One of them was always absent, and wandered about amongst the different German general-managers, from whom, however, it always returned home safely, like Noah's dove to the ark, certainly without an olive or laurel branch; then the next manuscript commenced its wanderings with similar result. Happily the composer, in addition to his talents and his scores, still possessed a few hundred thousand dollars, so that society could pardon his musical tendencies and performances. Long since he had bought himself a superb *bâton* in order one day to conduct one of his operas. With this magic staff in his pocket, Müller von Stallupönen, as he called himself, in order to be distinguished from other celebrated Müllers, ran about that day to make the necessary arrangements, his long hair fluttering in the breeze, which blew from off the East Sea. In spite of this cooling element, he was obliged to wipe the perspiration from his forehead, because it was a toilsome labour to obtain an equal temperature of disposition in all the coadjutors, and similarity of views about the pieces of music to be performed. The violoncellist as future diplomatist, supported him therein with valuable assistance. The little doctor proved to be the most obdurate, he maintained his opinion immovably as though it were some consultation beside a sick-bed. A mixed choral song was also contemplated. In that the fair sex must be especially begged for their co-operation, so as to give a graceful counter-balance to the rough, beery student voices of a few lawyers. The conductor moved about in most amiable *gracioso* from one seaside beauty to another, after having first brushed into order his hair which had been blown about by the sea-breeze. Although this amendment only remained effectual for a short time, still he appeared to advantage before the natural *coiffures* of most of the land-nymphs who allowed their loosened plaits, which had been dipped in the ocean's waves, to hang down their shoulders to dry. Both the Fräuleins von Dornau, of whom Olga had an imposing alto, Cäcilie a brilliant soprano voice at their disposal, had already made the musical agent happy with their consent, and his next move was to the Baute family, where he might hope for a rich musical harvest amongst the seven daughters.

But music's sister-art, poetry, which had not yet been proclaimed as its Siamese twin, as it was later in the artistic works of the future, must not be omitted. For Neukuhren possessed a much-made-of visitor in the young poet Schöner, who on this occasion must tune his lyre, all the more so because he was a friend of the young betrothed. Her engagement was really tantamount to a refusal for him, and it was a strange suggestion that he should celebrate that refusal with his poetical flowers; but Eva belonged already to his recollections, his love for her was now but a poetical page in his album; the renunciation was no longer hard for him. But another difficulty arose, his muse which was accustomed to sing the dawn of day on the political horizon, and the resurrection of nations, was not adapted for such domestic events; he could not discover the right key for it, such social and drawing-room poetry was not worthy of him, and reduced him to despair. He sprang up from his work-table and with hurried steps walked up and down the room. When he began to compose about roses, he always thought of the sword beneath the roses, the sword of Harmodius and Aristogiton, that he loved to wield in verse against all tyrants, and that which he was used to sing of passion's devouring flames was not fitted for a bridal idyll.

Schöner was obliged to curb his glowing fancy.

At last he had managed to produce a marriage poem, but when he read it over, he was alarmed at the reminiscences of the bridesmaids' wreath of violet silk which had slipped in. Schiller certainly had created no master-piece when he addressed Demoiselle Slevoigt in a nuptial poem—

"Zieh holde Braut mit unserm Segen,
Zieh hin auf Hymen's Blumenwegen."

Yet a few verses reminded one of that poem, and "the wreath's solemn adornment" had passed unnoticed in his ode. He tore it up angrily, rushed out into the air, and implored the Muses for only a few original ideas, that would be suitable for such a purpose, which the most commonplace mortals do not lack, if ever on a similar occasion they mount their Pegasus. The superabundance of genius with which he was endowed weighed heavily upon him, he longed for the intellectual level of an impromptu poet, who could daily shake a wedding ode out of his sleeve. The collegian Salomon was going about at the same time with the criminal thought of also reciting a sonnet, that he hoped to put together out of Heine and his extracts, and which should not be so harmless as an every-day congratulatory poem; he wanted to introduce a meaning, a fine poisoned meaning, which should only be comprehensible to the bride, which he intended to plunge into her heart like a vengeful dagger. In a lonely hollow walk, overgrown with sting-nettles he scanned the deadly verses on his fingers, until the murderous iambus flowed evenly upon its four feet without a halting choliambus. Had not Archilochos written satirical iambi the unhappy objects of which had hanged themselves in despair, what result might not be attained by a similar poetical production? What an effect, if he presented a bouquet to the bride-elect and a wasp flew out of it into her face, furnished with a sting such as Alphonse Karr's *guèpes* possessed, which at that time were so much liked by him!

As the arts, so was also the study of nature called into request, so as not to be wanting at the bridal ovation. A physician worked earnestly at the most uncertain of all studies, that of the weather, and gazed hopefully at the two barometers which he had brought with him to discover whether, in the evening, the full moon which was astronomically assured, might not be overcast by clouds of rain, and whether the dance could be carried out beneath the pear tree undisturbed by events of nature.

Doctor Reising and his Euphrasia had been towed back by her jealous sisters to the family table. They arrived exactly at the exciting moment in which Herr von Blanden introduced his betrothed.

Father Baute, who easily confused his daughters' names, was supported by Doctor Kuhl, the latter, alarmed at no feminine plural, calling out one after another as if at muster-roll.

Eva felt strange amongst all the strange faces. None was capable of inspiring her with immediate interest. Even the prettiest of the daughters, Lori, had a watchful smile that betokened mischief.

Blanden's invitation was accepted with many thanks. Hardly had he retired with his betrothed before the Baute family started noisily out of the respectful silence with which they had listened to the strange gentleman's words, and suddenly resembled a swarming bee-hive.

All talked at once. "How do you like her? How do you like him?" Those were the most coherent words which echoed simultaneously from all sides. Lori's sharp voice was the first to pierce through the noise.

"She cannot long have left her governesses. She is a very nice child, but the schoolroom clings to all her movements. He is a very different man. He shows plainly that he has long since passed through school, and also the school of life."

"She has fine eyes," said Ophelia, opening her own widely.

"But not so fine as yours," said Lori, quickly, "as that is all that you wished to hear."

"T could not like him," said Marie, "he looks so sleepy."

"That indicates a deep, mental life," said Euphrasia; "when he does open his eyes, a great deal of intellect lies in them. And he does open them when anything arouses his sympathies. We all, of course, are very uninteresting to him, but I like men to whom we are, or appear so."

"Well, then, you have an extensive public upon whom to exercise your liking," said Lori.

Albertina interrupted a silence of some hours with the thoughtful words—

"Besides, he has a good figure."

"I imagine her to be most domestic," said Emma, "and that is the principal matter. She is sure to be at home beside the kitchen fire and the bread board, and look very pretty there, too. And that is very important. It is no art to look well in a ball dress."

"My dear Emma," interposed Lori, "that is exactly true art! With the aid of paint, rouge, and the sculpture of a laced bodice, one must become a work of art."

"The bride-elect pleases me," said old Baute, wiping his spectacles, "she is natural," added he, with a melancholy glance at his daughters.

Herbart once maintained that everybody at certain points feels cramped by society. Professor Baute often, in the midst of his daughters, had this sensation of being cramped.

"There is something pleasant about her, and certainly it is a healthy nature.

She possesses repose and equanimity, and as thus the mutual determination of all ideas is connected through one another, she will also be sensible, she will not give way too much either to strong or weak affections; I believe we may congratulate this Blanden. He himself, however, appears to be of a passionate nature. But passions arise from an immoderately strong or ill-connected mass of conceptions. There are eulogists of passion. But, according to Herbart's and my view, it stands in repulsive contrast to all that really belongs to the well-being of mankind. Passion plays a great part in history. Herbart cautions us against charging the all-providing spirit of the universe with this part, it would otherwise resemble Mephistopheles too closely."

Doctor Reising's lips quivered convulsively; he passed his hand through his hair, and, as soon as Baute again wiped his spectacles, he broke forth indignantly with the words—

"False, all false! How beautifully Hegel says, it is the cunning of Reason that makes use of the passions of mankind for its own purposes. Without passion, nothing great can be done in the world. It is a narrow view that condemns passion because the compass of its wisdom is disturbed thereby."

Euphrasia ventured to touch the fanatical private tutor's coat sleeve in a beseeching manner. Reising understood the slight warning, and tried to stem the storm of indignation which had taken possession of him. But Baute said, with great composure—

"Any one who would solve the difficult question according to the causes of negative judgment, must look upon you, dear Reising, as an original phenomenon."

The young philosopher did not appear to be dissatisfied with the character assigned to him. He sat down, and pressed Euphrasia's hand underneath the table.

"In one thing I quite agree with you," said he, in a conciliatory tone, "my dear Professor, that Fräulein Kalzow is a truly harmonious looking creature. She is a beautiful, inspired, intellectually animated being."

Euphrasia considered it incumbent upon her to intimate to her future bridegroom her disapproval of such remarks by a pressure of her foot, which exceeded any expression of love.

"There is something of the beauty and repose about her," continued Reising, "something of the blissful majesty and winning loveliness which is peculiar to a classical ideal."

"Now that is too bad," said Lori, "did he ever utter such absurdities to us? Pray do not forget that we, too, are classical in our way."

"The infatuation of men!" said Ophelia, "anything new always possesses a most bewitching charm for them."

Euphrasia had risen poutingly, and crushed her straw hat in her hand; tall Albertina drew aside from the Doctor as from a criminal. War with all the daughters had succeeded the peace which he had just concluded with the father.

Reising, however, assumed an air of being unconscious of this outlawry which could be read on every countenance. He lighted a cigar, and stroked the large poodle which Professor Baute had procured in order to pursue a study of animals' souls, which, as a genuine Herbartian, he did not class very far beneath those of mankind.

Meanwhile, Blanden had seated himself in a distant arbour with Doctor Kuhl. Their conversation also turned upon Eva.

"She is also a Principessa," said Kuhl, "and may any day compete with the fairy of Lago Maggiore as regards the magic of her beauty. I wish you joy from my heart, dear friend."

"And I feel my happiness, perfectly, fully! It seems to me as if I had previously only seen the world through a veil, as if I now saw it clearly and steadily in free and yet decided outlines. All gloomy over-cloudings of my life have been transformed into sunny vapour, such as lies upon a bright landscape."

"Indeed, she will relieve Kulmitten from its everlasting tedium," said Kuhl. "A splendid estate, but there in those woods one must become melancholy; a covey of wild ducks across the yawning lake alone brings animation into the lifeless scene. But will she like it?"

"My dear friend, a young wife—"

"Shall live entirely in her husband, I know. But besides that devout worship, she needs fresh air and sunshine, nor are we indeed gods. Concerts, theatres, all favourite resources she must dispense with there."

"She will know how to adapt herself to it; domestic happiness—"

"Now you are beginning to preach! You know desperately little of that happiness so far; a remedy whose efficacy you have not tried yourself, without hesitation you calmly prescribe for your wife."

"You see everything in a gloomy light to-day."

"I am not in rosy mood; I, too, have my little annoyances. You will be happy, I hope, but what may lie dormant in your wife, who can tell? They often change wonderfully after marriage. Every Pandora, however beautiful she is, has her box that is filled with evil, and only when she is married does she raise the cover."

"Those are consoling reflections for a lover."

"She is beautiful, really beautiful, but she has such enthusiastic eyes. There is something insatiable about all enthusiasm. She will, perhaps, love you, but she will demand of you that you shall have none other thought besides her; she will desire to be everything to you, house and court, state and church, society and philosophy, extract of all beauty and amiability that exists on earth. Quintescence of all intellectual advantages that are usually divided amongst various talents, she will be jealous of the book that you read, of the woman to whom you speak, of the friend to whom you pour out your heart; for anything that I know, even of me. *Dixi et animam salvi*," said the inexorable Doctor, as he pressed his felt hat farther over his brow.

At that moment, Wegen came up breathlessly, a packet of letters under his arm. Kuhl responded coldly and glumly to his friendly greeting.

"All goes well," cried Blanden's factotum, that cheery friend, whose cheeks sea air and zeal had combined to redden. "Müller von Stallupönen is getting a first-rate orchestra together; this evening a grand rehearsal. The mixed chorus is formed; I, too, sing in it. We shall only have a couple of light, lively songs; there is not time enough to bring up the heavy guns; it would take too much trouble. Some of the male singers have no ears, some of the female ones no voices, and Müller, as conductor, will be able to wield his ivory *bâton*, with its silver mounting, just as well. Müller is a good leader, but very rude. People's position is nothing to him; he treats ladies of the greatest importance as a policeman would women who were obstructing the way. If we had to learn a difficult vocal piece, there would be more actions for damages than notes. But I must away, my good friend."

"I am very grateful to you for your zeal, dear Wegen; but whither are you going in such haste?" asked Blanden.

"You see I am freighted with music; I am going to Fräulein Cäcilie von Dornau. She will sing a solo, and I shall accompany her, but we have not yet decided what we shall select."

Doctor Kuhl's fingers drummed impatiently upon the table.

"I have searched out every note that was to be met with amongst the principal stars in the heaven of the Neukuhren musicians, and also amongst the Baute Pleiaides; besides that, I have plundered all pianos and music cupboards. But I must away, Fräulein Cäcilie expects me."

Wegen bade adieu as breathlessly and hastily as he had arrived. Blanden looked smilingly at the Doctor, who now sat there with moody glances and folded arms.

"But tell me, friend, what does this signify? It almost looks as if it were impious desecration of your sanctuary. Does the flame of the Dioscuri no longer shine at the mast of your life's ship? Cäcilie, the beloved one of your intellectual days, appears to have become faithless to you."

"It is possible," replied the Doctor.

"Friend Wegen at least moves briskly and cheerily in the channel of a new affection which is surely not to be discouraged, otherwise he would not be in so roseate an humour."

"I do not know if this Lacertes is escaping me," said Kuhl, with defiant resignation, "I do not know if it is in earnest or in play when she shows such particular attention to Herr von Wegen; I almost think she is playing with us both."

"Is she a coquette, then?"

"All are, women and girls, each in her own manner. I think she will make fun of me and my views. Yesterday I called her to account for her response to Herr von Wegen, and she excused herself with the most charming grace. She quite shared my views; life is much too rich to be able to restrict oneself; besides, nothing is so ridiculous as jealousy. She likes me much, but only on her intellectual days; therefore, for her foolish days, of which she experiences many now, she has sought out Herr von Wegen. And, at the same time, she smiled so politely, and made me such a pretty curtsey."

Blanden could not suppress loud merriment at this communication.

"She beats you with your own weapons."

"Laugh away! It drives me to despair! Who can explain to such a sprite, in solemn earnest, what a great difference exists between man and woman in restriction of the affections?"

"Nor would that be so easy."

"Simple as a child, I tell you, only I have no inclination to do so at present. Besides, I am curious to see how far she carries it."

"Perhaps to marriage. Our whole life is only directed towards that, and you always go groping about in an Utopia with your theories. But girls have sense and tact, and, at a certain age, they begin to freeze in the open air, and seek a shelter."

"I shall never believe that Cäcilie belongs to those everyday womanish natures; but if she be really in earnest with this Herr von Wegen, I shall know how to console myself. For a rejected lover, there is often nothing more consolatory than the thought of his successor, for if the latter belongs to tin soldiers, a man knows, too, in which box he must pack his beloved one, and that he has been much mistaken if he counted her amongst living ones. An error is always painful, but it is a pleasure to find it out; the table must be entirely cleared and laid again from the beginning."

"Do not forget that Wegen is my friend," said Blanden, seriously.

"As a friend, he may possess great merits. I appreciate his self-sacrificing zeal; but in a girl, who can be in love with him, I have been mistaken, and that is my affair. Now farewell, I must go into the sea! They are tuning the fiddles over there already. I shall get out of the way of that *dilettante* howling to-day."

While Kuhl walked, towards the bathing-place, Blanden went in search of his betrothed. However, the old Regierungsrath, whose countenance was now filled with unwonted sunshine, informed him that Eva had begged to be allowed to be quite alone that evening. There were evenings on which she loved to indulge her thoughts in solitude, and she hoped her *fiancé* would grant her that privilege once more on the evening before her betrothal.

Kalzow declared himself ready to compensate the lonely lover with a game of *ombre*, at which the Kreisgerichtsrath would assist, and even a "dummy" was provided, if he should appear to be necessary.

The only young man in Kuhren available, was one who neither sang nor played upon any instrument, the talented architect, who, on that evening, would certainly have to sit as "dummy" at all the concert rehearsals.

Blanden assented unwillingly; he was full of ardent yearning for his betrothed; the wish to see her, to speak to her, being ungratified, became all the keener in him. How pale appeared the picture that his imagination sketched of the beautiful girl. It alarmed him that the outlines sometimes seemed to become confused, and out of that dimness another picture gazed towards him, which had once been dear to his heart.

He sat down to *ombre*, but his thoughts were absent. He held the most beautiful *soli* in his hand and forgot to declare them. Close by, the noisy orchestral rehearsal was in full swing. These mangled pieces of music, which Müller von Stallupönen's zeal tore into single bars, appeared like mockery to him; these discordant, disconnected instruments, moved *en echelon* when they ought to march in line.

But yet this rehearsal was arranged to prepare a performance in his honour, and how dreadful the dissonances that were thus disclosed.

Eva meanwhile sat in her room, which was illumined by the moon, meditating quietly and deeply. All who are completely absorbed in another's or their own life, are filled with intense melancholy. Whether the destinies be sad or bright, their lot always seems worthy of tears. Yesterday is a dream, to-morrow a question, to-day an uncertain possession. It is always difficulty to believe in any great felicity in this world, so abundant in delusions!

How brightly life lay before her! She, the betrothed of a beloved man of position, of a respected and rich landowner—what had befallen that shy Eva? What will her school-friends say to this transformation of fortune? From her adopted father's four narrow walls, she was transported into a circle in which she could shine, as well as command and influence. But if, in meditating, these thoughts and fancies just touched her mind, they wore but the gorgeous setting for the picture of the man to whom her heart had given itself fully and wholly, whom she would have followed in poverty and want, yes, even unto death!

It was an overwhelming passion that she cherished for Blanden; she was almost alarmed at it and her own heart. Was she, then, worthy to be this excellent man's wife? Amidst tears, she looked into the mirror, and if she found those features lovely whose reflex gazed upon her, doubly lovely in the halo of transfiguration which intense emotion shed upon her, above all she was filled with joy that she was richly dowered with beauty and charm for him.

And how should she cheer him! The gloomy line had not escaped her which lay upon his forehead around his eyebrows, the pensive sadness in his half-closed eyes. Life had done him great injury; all this should be changed!

She felt the power within herself to keep spring-time awake in him; so mighty were the wish and will in her. And for her, too, what nameless bliss! What unknown enchantments the future concealed for her in its lap! How she had thrilled at his ardent kisses! Like the evening's glow from golden clouds, a dream-like fire had flowed towards her. She plunged below into the flames, and the flames did not scorch nor burn her, but pressed themselves around her limbs with a hitherto unknown feeling of ecstasy and sweet enchantment.

And yet she became so feverishly hot in that dream! She threw the window open; without, all lay calmly and indifferently in the silvery coolness of the moonlight. The waves broke upon the shore as they had done since the beginning of time, unconcerned in the troubles and joys of men, and only the agonised notes of unperfected music that seemed to quiver convulsively beneath the conductor's *bâton*, reminded her, as they fell upon her ears from the Kurhans, of human life and her own betrothal feast.

She sat at the window, lost in thought. For simultaneously with the beloved man, another joy entered into her poor life. A touching vision bent over her; her tears flowed lightly.

The mother, who had so long been kept afar from her, was invited. She was sure to come to-morrow; could it have been a betrothal feast without her blessing? In the cold one of her adopted parents lay no charm which should be able to enchain her destiny; but a mother's every silent wish must become a blessing. How would she look now? Oh, to gaze again into those large, touching eyes, to be able to ask her why she had remained so far away from her daughter; to be able to comfort her, if she had endured great sorrow—and certainly she must be unhappy! The wicked world had made her so! All pictures of early childhood rose again before her, dream-like, unconnectedly. Yet from none was her mother's countenance absent. Here they sat in an arbour before a coffee-table, and the mother drove away the wasps which tried to steal the little daughter's cake; there she stood at a door, behind the curtained glass panes of which the lights of a Christmas tree were already gleaming impatiently. She beckoned and called, and all the festive brilliancy which had delighted the child's heart reflected itself in the mother's eyes, and as she embraced the latter, the never-to-be-forgotten tears that she kissed away from those cheeks told her how intensely she was beloved by the only one who watched over her life like the eye of Providence! And again she saw herself in a large park. The mother sat upon a bench, and worked; it was already dusk. Eva could even now still transport herself entirely into the feelings of that time—what fear she was in lest her mother might spoil her beautiful eyes. She cautioned her dear mother, and sprang to the pond close by—the lights of evening flickered—a splendid water lily attracted her— Evchen stooped down to gather it, and sank into the pond. A cry for help— she awoke in her mother's arms, who had torn her quickly as lightning from out the waves. As she opened her eyes, she looked into a face smiling beneath its tears; and often in her dreams appeared her mother's picture, as it had stood before her at that moment.

Infinite yearning, deep emotion, took possession of her; how abundant was her mother's love, and who had parted her from her daughter, wrenched her away from that child's heart? She felt that it was not the mother's will; a dark, spectre-like secret had stepped between the two! Yet separated, even from a distance, the mother watched over her life, reckoning up hour after hour of her present and future, and adding them together in one single divine thought of illimitable love!

Sobbing loudly, she rested her head upon her hand; her eyes did not see the heavens above, nor the wide ocean—only her mother's picture.

Then she suddenly arose; why this sorrow before a day of joy? To-morrow the sun illumines their reunion, to-morrow she gives her troth to the beloved man; she will sleep and dream of all her approaching happiness.

The sounds of music had long been hushed, but through the window rang the thunder of the sea; it increased with the growing storm. The hoarse breaking of the waves rocked Eva to sleep; but it was a sleep full of fear, and a distant angry destiny, into which the noise of the waves was changed, broke menacingly into her dreams.

CHAPTER XII.

UNDER THE PEAR TREE.

Kuhl was no friend of betrothal and marriage feasts; he thought such customs should be left to the savage races of people. For educated human beings it was most unseemly to announce such quiet secret happiness to towns and villages as if with the beating of drums. That eccentric man, therefore, experienced deep dissatisfaction at the festive mood in which all Neukuhren rejoiced on his friend's betrothal day, and sought the most lonely paths on the strand in order to escape the noise of preparations and arrangements. This was not easy; for the great kettle-drum having once been called into requisition, it shook the atmospherical waves on every side at the incessant musical rehearsals, and strove to out-do the roaring of the billows.

That Cäcilie should also take part in these rehearsals, and probably practise her vocal solo with Wegen, did not conduce to improve his humour. He had become more indifferent to Olga during those days; was he not certain of her love. She was all devotion, and, as of old, had an approving smile for his most daring flights of thought; but that fugitive, smooth as an eel, occupied all his thoughts, and strengthened the ill-temper to which he gave himself up so recklessly.

Wegen meanwhile was ubiquitous; now he sat at the piano and accompanied Cäcilie, then he stood by the carts full of evergreens and overlooked the decorations of the room. The Chief Forester, who was a friend of Blanden's, and who was expected on that evening, had proved himself particularly helpful in supplying garlands of leaves and flowers. Then again Wegen, with a powerful telling tenor, gave decision and firmness to the choruses, and during the pauses he might be seen outside under the pear tree where he had the nature's carpet of the dancing ground swept by the fair sex of the village. The entire programme of the entertainment lay in his hands, he was assisted in the arrangements by the future diplomatist, who, as Wegen's aide-de-camp, sped hither and thither in equally feverish activity.

The physician declared himself to be perfectly satisfied with the weather; steady, immovable sunshine was extended over land and sea, and similar excellent intentions might be expected of the full moon. And like the sky, Müller von Stallupönen displayed a contented smile the livelong day. The orchestra surpassed all anticipation, and even the second violins, whose notes were always dragging behind the rest, had gradually settled down into correct time. The vocal choruses also roused the master's satisfaction, but this had not been attained without dogged interference with the rights of personal liberty. A first lieutenant's widow and an unmarried young lady of noble birth in the neighbourhood, whose love for the glorious art of song was an unhappy one, had proved themselves impervious to the whole *crescendo* of insults which had been rained upon them from the conductor's desk, and continued with lamentable obstinacy to sow the tares of false notes amongst the wheat of the otherwise superb choral singing. No other means remained but to have recourse to violent measures, and to exclude the two ladies positively from the body of musical members. They deemed it impossible to survive this insult in Neukuhren, and on the same afternoon they migrated to the neighbouring watering-place Rauschen, and in such haste that the first lieutenant's widow actually forgot to pay her bills.

Professor Baute's poodle had caused another disturbance; when accompanied by his master, he had attended one of the rehearsals, at the room door he suddenly began to bark, and indeed with all the eagerness of an art-enthusiast. Baute pacified him for a time, but as the dog again unbridled his enthusiasm, the director made a deferential observation, which obliged the poodle and his master to leave the room door. This was very disagreeable for the professor, as he was just engaged in an examination as to which series of ideas were awakened by music in an animal's soul, thus causing the dog to bark.

The excitement in Neukuhren, and the want of time were so great that on this day even sea bathing was forgotten. The bathing-woman could record that with the exception of Fräulein Olga von Dornau, who did not permit herself to be disturbed in her habits of life, and would not be deprived of such daily strengthening of her immaculate health for the most important occurrences, not one woman plunged into the waves of the East Sea on that day.

Evening drew on, the full moon's pale outlines in the sky gained a clearer form as the sun went down, from a cloud it became a planet. The room resembled a meadow, upon which had bloomed the gayest field and woodland flowers mostly in light colours, the Baute family especially appeared like a prismatic rainbow.

Light summer robes, and rigorous ball dresses floated about amongst one another; Olga wore a ball dress that was cut out in Court style, and displayed her voluptuous beauty; Cäcilie on the other hand a summer dress close to the neck, but which, however, displayed her excessively slight waist most daintily.

The Chief Forester created some sensation amongst the guests by his giant form and abundant white moustache. Although he was well up in years, he carried himself with military erectness, and the powerful tone of his voice awoke the envy of all the basses in the chorus. Blanden had greeted him with special cordiality, for the latter had been his father's dearest friend. The young man looked with emotion at the worthy forest official's grey head, he felt as though the former represented his father to-day, and shook him congratulatorily by the hand. Already during the afternoon Professor Baute had contemplated with great interest the huge bull-dog which the Chief Forester brought with him, and with his hero's assistance had made its acquaintance. He had already noted several particular tokens of intelligence, for the bull-dog clearly occupied a higher position in the scale of animal's souls than his own poodle.

Wegen had caused a couple of garlanded chairs to be placed upon a small daïs for the betrothed couple; the other guests sat beside it—elderly gentlemen and ladies and all those who lacked the muse of the art of sweet sounds.

Eva, accompanied by her adopted parents, appeared in a simple blue dress, a wreath of wild flowers in her hair, and amongst them gleamed the bells of the campanula. What a contrast between her dress and the townish splendour with which Frau Kalzow had decked herself, even several doubtful diamonds were not missing. The satin rustled around her stalwart but bony form, as if in wondering amazement, and as though it did not belong to her. The old Regierungsrath had brought out his stiffest neckcloth at the same time as his most solemn demeanour; every movement told how nearly this festivity concerned him, and what reflected rays of importance it shed upon his poor self. But it was not merely in her simple dress that Eva's beauty possessed such a touching charm. Intense mournfulness that alternated with suddenly aroused eagerness overspread her countenance. She had been expecting her mother's arrival during the whole day, she had rushed in feverish haste to the window as each carriage drove up to the Kursaal, and the futility of this incessant agitation acted depressingly and paralysingly at last, so that several times she burst into tears. Frau Kalzow consoled her with saying her mother might still come; she was written to punctually, and at the proper time, it was possible that the letter by some mischance might not have arrived equally punctually. She did not dare to think of any illness, they would surely have received the intelligence by writing. Nevertheless, to the bride the whole betrothal ceremony appeared upset and saddened by her mother's absence. The good wishes of her women friends offered little compensation for it, they were mostly but the friends of yesterday. Kanzleirath's Minna spoke hers really most honestly; she liked Blanden, too, but she was too phlegmatic to be jealous, and too good natured not to give her best wishes to every bride upon her path through life.

The room had filled, the village inhabitants pressed around the open doors, some of the village beauties were invited to the dance beneath the pear tree. The orchestra commenced the overture to *Der Freischütz*. While one portion of the householders and fishermen of the place listened attentively to the music, the others were drawn away by an unhoped for distraction, because in the garden outside, Doctor Kuhl amused himself in making Nero and the Forester's bull-dog compete in jumping over tables and benches, while he declined the delights of the music in a defiant manner. Only when the spirit-like tremolo of the "Waldschlucht" had died away and a voice began to sing the Erl-king to a pianoforte accompaniment, did Kuhl push a table outside against the window, spring on to it with both dogs, and between the poodle and bull-dog listened devoutly to his Cäcilie's song, for it was she who, accompanied by Wegen, executed Schubert's entrancing melody with more passion than he had given her credit for. When the orchestra then played Haydn's Symphony in C sharp, Kuhl sprang down again from his improvised opera-box, and indulged in gymnastic amusements such as are seen at fairs and annual markets, gradually drawing the interest of the public standing outside completely away from the dream world of music. Even the choruses of Mendelssohn's songs, "Come fly with me and be my wife," and "There fell a frost at midnight's hour," could only rouse the athletic doctor to momentary attention. "That Müller von Stallupönen," he muttered to himself, "has already let a frost at midnight fall upon the flowers of the betrothal-day; what icy cold will reign later on at that hour!"

Eva sat, stirred with silent emotion, on the decorated chair. So often as the door was opened, when a late comer arrived, she turned her glance in that direction, and sprang up from her seat several times, as if she expected to greet her mother in each lady who entered. Blanden even perceived her agitation; he enquired its cause, but she did not venture to confess to him that even on this day she still yearned for another person, for her mother. Had he not listened very indifferently to a conversation in which she mentioned her mother, and, as it appeared, had intentionally broken it off; yes, a friend even told her she had heard him say to Doctor Kuhl, when passing by, he had quite enough with one mother-in-law.

At the conclusion, Müller von Stallupönen had arranged for an overture of his own composition to be performed by his orchestra. What young composer would allow such a rare opportunity to escape of calling his musical conceptions into life with real instruments? Blanden and Eva thanked him politely for that symphony which, from henceforth, he christened the

"Betrothal symphony," and intended to issue to the world under that title. The audience of visitors had applauded briskly, it is true, but had really found the deep thoughtfulness of the composition very tedious. The unlearned lovers of music especially wondered at it; they like to carry some tune home with them. For the abundant counter-point and fugues which worked most artistically into and amongst one another, debarred any one from reaching the enjoyment of that transitory and despised foam which many half-cultivated people designate as melody, and which they would gladly extract as easily gained from the vast undulations of a musical genius penetrating into the depths.

Now a brilliant entertainment commenced; Blanden and Wegen did the honours. Eva sat beside Cäcilie, to whom she confidentially communicated her hopes and fears; that astute Fräulein von Dornau was not at a loss for reasons with which to pacify the betrothed. Nevertheless, the latter could not attain a happy state of mind.

"Just look at Evchen," said Lori to her sister Euphrasia. "Does not the poor child glance incessantly at the door, as if she expected a ghost, or some former lover, who would put his veto upon this new betrothal?"

"Indeed, in this mixed company," said Euphrasia, "one might easily imagine oneself transported to a Polish diet, where such 'vetoes' are the order of the day."

"Cäcilie comforts the poor child," said Lori. "She reposes upon her laurels. Did you not remark how, when performing the Erl-king, she looked down upon Herr von Wegen's rather light-coloured head, and with peculiar fervour, at the words: 'I love you; I'm charmed with your beautiful form?'"

"Olga," said Emma, "meanwhile enjoys herself intensely at the supper-table; she has drawn her chair as closely as possible to the roasted capercailzie, and does her duty by the sweets."

"I believe," said Lori, "that girl has really no soul; she is an Undine, but of that vigorous species which is only to be found splashing about at sea-side watering-places. Her body is a dense veil that hangs around her soul."

"This is a very democratic affair," said the Regierungsrath, as he pledged the Kreisgerichtsrath in a glass of Madeira. "My son-in-law enjoys that; I do not like losing myself thus amongst subordinates."

"My old friend," replied the other, "what harm have those two innocent Secretaries, who enjoy their life here, done to you? You can never take the cap-button, of which Herr von Blanden told us so amusingly, with you into the bath below."

"You are an incorrigible democrat," replied Kalzow, annoyed.

Spirits still rose; the attornies begged the young ladies for dances under the pear tree. One of them had invited the seven Fräuleins von Baute, one after another, and had their names written down upon his dancing-card; his friends designated him the possessor of the seven evil spirits.

Father Baute, meanwhile, had forced young Doctor Reising into a corner, and declared to him, with elevated champagne glass, that he now boldly challenged the latter to any discussion, as his ideas stepped more briskly than ever across the threshold of consciousness, while Reising, on the contrary, also excited by wine, protested in permitting himself the daring utterance that consciousness has no threshold, because it has not been made by any carpenter, and indeed that mode of philosophising always caused him to imagine himself transported to some mental timber yard, as, for example, when the formation of ideas was talked of.

But the Professor became beside himself; with a wide sweeping movement, he dashed the champagne glass into pieces against the wall.

"You say that to a disciple of Herbart; incredible!"

Reising, who had long since been shocked at his own daring, hardly knew how to shield himself from the Professor's furious wrath.

Euphrasia, whose entire future threatened to fall into broken potsherds, approached the opponents, wringing her hands.

Doctor Kuhl's interposition was more powerful; he thrust his Herculean form between them.

"Peace, sirs! '*In vino veritas*? said one Roman; but 'what is truth!' said another Roman. Here there is certainly no time to fathom it. Look, Fräulein Euphrasia appears as an angel of peace; true womanliness was even able to redeem a thinker like Faust. Let the flag of peace be waved! We will drink to an alliance between Hegel and Herbart. Neither Napoleon nor German philosophy ever recognised anything to be impossible."

The Kursaal, like Westminster Abbey, possessed a Poet's Corner in which the admired poet, Schöner, was obliged to permit himself to be instructed by the school-boy, Salomon, on several important questions concerning the art of poesy. Salomon had strengthened the consciousness of his intellectual superiority with several glasses of champagne, and could not resist pointing out to Poet Schöner, despite all recognition of his talents, that political lyrics were an unlawful hermaphrodite species of poetry, inasmuch as one is always led away to subjects about which leading articles appear in the newspapers. What a totally different influence a song of Heine or Eichendorff possesses: "*In einem kühlen Grunde, da geht ein Mühlenrad.*"

"The mill wheel in the cool valley, my friend," said Schöner, as he patted the young connoisseur upon his shoulders with the air of a protector, "goes round in our heads too long already, and the German people become so stupid with all that folly, so stupid—let us drink to your well-being, young poet!"

The glasses clinked. Immediately afterwards both poets relapsed into deep silence, for each mutely recited the verses which he intended to declaim under the pear tree. There the betrothal should be proclaimed before all the assembly, and then only Schöner and Salomon proposed bringing their Pegasus into action in the arena.

Wegen announced to the hero of the day that all was in readiness outside. Indeed, merry sounds of village music soon made themselves heard, which several amateurs and the big kettle drum had joined in the highest spirits.

The village population moved merrily about. Beside the flags of the village school, others fluttered, which the watering-place visitors had hastily improvised. Yes, Doctor Kuhl had even requisitioned the large one which was hoisted in order to prohibit bathing when the sea was tempestuous, and this flag, which he never respected, he now bore with Herculean strength before the procession. The latter had soon been got into order. Behind Kuhl came the musicians, who had been joined by numerous girls from the village, with wreaths and garlands. Then followed the betrothed couple, behind them the parents, then Wegen with Cäcilie, Reising with Euphrasia, and other pairs, just as they chanced to find themselves together, or according to previous agreement had joined one another. Singing merry popular songs, the sailors and fishermen, with wives and daughters, followed in a noisy throng.

Thus the procession moved towards the big pear tree. The light of the full moon lay upon the sea and the shore, the sky was glittering with stars, the sounds of music awoke the distant echoes.

Eva leaned against Blanden in a feeling of silent beatitude, such as she had not known during the whole day; now she thought only of her beloved one and the future; in that moment she forgot her mother! Was not all the rejoicing of these jubilant beings meant for her alone; in honour of her happiness the music rang, the flags waved—all was festively adorned.

"Oh, my beloved," she said to Blanden, "to you I owe all this bliss! We will be happy, as happy for ever, as at this moment."

"My sweet girl!" replied Blanden, pressing her to his heart, "I, too, feel now as if there were no discords upon earth—despite the village music," added he, with that variable humour, the play of whose thoughts he could never control. "But, indeed, nothing is so touching as the people's pleasure, however it may express itself. So much sadness lies concealed behind this joy; all the labour of dull, dreary days, all the struggle to make life bearable for themselves, so much external want, and many an internal grief, which affects them doubly painfully in that want. What, in comparison, is the delusive happiness of a joyous moment? And because this happiness is short and delusive, it disposes one to sadness."

"Why these melancholy thoughts?" said Eva, "why think of others to-day? We will care for them all our life, mitigate every want, whenever we encounter them—this I have vowed to myself; but, on this one day, we have the right to think only of ourselves, to give ourselves up alone to the feeling of blissful enjoyment."

"That will we; you are right! Do I not hear, amidst the loud music, the quiet blue forest bells ring harmoniously, fairy-like, my lovely campanula! It is a wedding-march of the elves, that only my ear perceives, for what does the world comprehend of the midsummer night's dream that we dream together?"

Meanwhile, the procession had arrived at the pear tree, and merry tunes were played upon the dancing ground above which the moon's rays flickered.

Village beauties and lady visitors whirled round in gay confusion; even father Baute joined the dances, while Reising, uninitiated in that art, leaned somewhat annoyedly against the old tree's stem. In vain Euphrasia and her six sisters invited him to dance, and Lori and the little ones could not suppress a few ill-natured remarks, which were pointed at the young philosopher's awkwardness.

Blanden perceived, with supreme satisfaction, that the old Chief Forester opened the dance with Eva; that worthy man, with silvery beard and the iron cross upon his breast, gave to Blanden's young love the blessing of the older generation, which, in his own house had become extinct.

But for his present struggles, this venerable man was a beautiful example. Even if he could not attain the fearlessness of such a sterling nature after spending his life in such wild storms, he could strive to follow it in steady labour and work, and, like the Forester in his calling, stand firmly in doing active good.

The music made a pause. Kalzow cleared his throat; he felt that the moment for the announcement of the betrothal had arrived. Arm in arm, Blanden and Eva were still resting from the last dance. Then the gentle roll of wheels upon the soft grass roused their attention. A carriage drew up; a lady descended and approached the dancing ground through the opening rows of people.

A white veil, which intercepted the moonlight in a spectre-like manner, still concealed her features.

Eva's heart beat violently, she released herself from her future bridegroom's arms, and extended her own to the strange figure.

There could be no doubt; she it was, who was expected so ardently. Then the stranger threw back her veil; the moon lay full upon refined but ghastly pale features. Two large eyes, dimmed with tears, rested with intense pain, like two stars of evil boding, upon the youthful, beautiful form that hastened to meet her with all the eagerness of love.

Soon Eva lay upon her mother's heart; in intense rapture, both forgot the staring crowd.

"How beautiful you have become!" whispered the mother, as she stroked her daughter's hair and cheeks, buried herself in those gazelle-like eyes, encircled that slender waist with her arms, "and taller than I!"

"And you still look so young, dear mother, you might be my sister."

"I am rather late. An accident befell the carriage; it broke a wheel. I still do not know whether I come to you with a blessing or a curse."

"A curse, mother?" Eva asked fearfully.

"And yet—that one went away, far away into the world," said she, as if speaking to herself. "The family is large; they are the same names."

Meanwhile, Kalzow had drawn near, and received his sister with a solemn embrace, while Miranda contented herself with offering the tips of her right hand fingers in sisterly welcome.

Blanden had vouchsafed less attention to this meeting than might have been expected.

He had once entertained unorthodox views about mothers-in-law; would neither disturb the daughter's nor the relatives' greeting, and, remaining averted, he conversed with Doctor Kuhl, who had just emptied a glass of punch, upon the strengthening properties of that beverage.

Thereupon, Eva went towards him, leading her mother by the hand.

"Max, my mother," said she, as she now left her mother and stood beside her lover.

She was about to utter his name, when the word died upon her lips.

Pale as death, with an expression of infinite pain, the mother swooned. Dr. Kuhl caught her in his arms, for Blanden stood as if motionless, staring at what seemed incredible to him. For a moment it appeared to him as if the sky, with all its stars, danced above him; as if this assembly adorned with flags, ribbons and garlands, was but a mirage, gliding down from out the clouds, and this strange, veiled, unconscious figure a ghost, that filled his soul with a shudder from the grave.

But though it all came over him with thoughts following quickly as lightning, like boundless pain, as though a yawning cleft went through his whole life—as though a ghost-like hand were thrusting him back when he hoped to attain peaceful bliss, and like the pressure of an ever-tightening rack, the thought suffused his whole soul that his betrothal was impossible.

And it was that, which the weak woman now raising herself, seemed to whisper into her brother's ear, who started back as if stung by an adder.

Tortured with unutterable fear, Eva hastened to and fro. Was that still the same glittering starlit sky, and the same moon-illumined world, still the same joyfully-excited crowd? The only sad secret of her life had risen up in all its magnitude, darkening everything, and casting unholy shadows upon the happiness of her love. The festive music, the merry circling dance, seemed to her like mockery. With ready presence of mind, Dr. Kuhl had given the signal for it to re-commence, so as not to interrupt the entertainment, and to conceal behind the enjoyment of the many, that mysterious, crushing occurrence.

"To-morrow, my daughter, to-morrow," said her mother, "to-day, I am ill, and will seek my room."

Eva looked round, as if imploring aid; all were silent on every side, and looked upon the ground; Blanden, too, was mute; not one comforting word that the betrothal should still be promulgated.

Was it then possible? Was it she herself—she—Eva Kalzow, the heroine of that day, the object of the congratulations, the fêted one, who must shrink away from this feast like a criminal, into whose face was cast the bridal wreath which had been snatched from her? What dishonourable deed had she committed? Did she not stand there as if in a pillory?

Did they not smile scornfully, maliciously—the seven Fräuleins Baute—at the interrupted feast? Did not her other female friends whisper mysteriously with speaking glances?

Impossible—it was a fevered dream, an agonising fevered dream—it could not be so.

What then has happened? With convulsive terror she thought of possibility after possibility—nothing remained for her but the dull weight of dismal, fearful foreboding.

Inquiringly she looked up at Kalzow; he shrugged his shoulders.

It was true, then, she was disgraced before everybody. With a heartrending cry she sank into her mother's arms.

"I shall follow you, mother!" cried she, in a tone of despairing resignation.

She turned towards Blanden; he came up to her, pressed her hands—she saw a tear in his eye.

"Good-night, Eva," said he, with overflowing emotion, in a suffocating voice.

"Good-night"—she felt as in a dream, where, wandering through subterranean passages, one door is shut noisily after another, and the sneck closes clatteringly—ever farther on into the deep abyss of night.

And no word of elucidation—all shared that secret—all kept silence, even he—was that his love?

Pressing her hand upon her heart, she followed her mother; she looked round once more.

There he stood, his tall figure drawn up erectly, his pale face seemed to quiver with some internal struggle. She forgot her own anguish in his. It was indeed impossible—he could not be lost to her.

The Kalzows and Blanden remained behind, so as not to interrupt the entertainment by a general departure. Kuhl had declared upon his honour that sudden indisposition on the part of the bride's mother had called the former away. Thus people did not allow themselves to be disturbed in their enjoyment, the bride was soon forgotten, as she was merely the chance cause of the gay evening dance. Only the two poets went about in a melancholy frame of mind; the unspoken verses of their *carmina* passed in pieces through their minds, and bitter regret for the laurels which the people of Neukuhren had turned for them, and of which they had been deprived, eat into their souls.

"What does all this mean?" Kuhl asked his friend.

"Follow me to my room, afterwards," replied Blanden.

Early morning which, on the summer's night, dawned with its first streaks of red on the horizon, only put an end to the enjoyment of the dancers.

In the deep silence of that early hour, which brings something sanctifying with it, after refreshing sleep, something gloomy after a watchful night, the two friends sat together in a comfortable room, looking over the wide ocean, whose waves seemed to thrill with kindling rapture at the first greeting of the young day's orb.

Kuhl had lighted a cigar, and with a cup of Mocca before him, he listened with unshaken equanimity to the disclosures of his nervously agitated friend.

END OF VOL. I.